BUBBLES FROM RUBBLES

AMARA CHIDINMA EZEDINIRU

&

VICTOR IBEH

For information visit:

http://www.amarainspires.com

Edited by Raymond Sefia
Book and Cover design by Fehintoluwa
Book Formatting by Tope Akintayo @TopeConsult
Published by Rald and Vid Consulting

1st Edition published November 2018

ISBN: 978-978-973-118-3

DEDICATION

To all single mothers who are yet to recover from the blows dealt by the choice of a partner, it's our hope that you will find what you seek.

To all those who are experiencing emotional upheaval, may your storm become calm soonest.

To those in the web of an abusive relationship, may you find strength to do what's best for you.

Acknowledgment

Our profound gratitude goes to Raymond J. Sefia for painstakingly going through this work.

+

Prologue

BUBBLES FROM RUBBLES IS A SEQUEL OF THE novel, *In and Out*, a story of delusional love.

Long after escaping from the abusive and controlling powers of a man, Ijendu remained imprisoned. Her actions and utterances did not depict a free woman. Even though Ijendu thought she was living the life, her life remained rudderless. Every time she thought she displayed respect for her values, she contradicted herself. No one believed her nor did they take her seriously. Not only did She sway from one side to the other with her actions, she also blew hot and cold with her words. Her unusual ways of thinking and behaving became glaring as the strength of her character was tested.

Ijendu was a victim of an unbalanced society where merit did not open the door and reason was scorned. Numerous times, she was a lone voice. Sometimes, she blended, other times, she weathered the storm. She scampered like a mouse in the trash of life. She doubted herself, her competence and everything about her. She was constantly reminded that she was out of prison. No one had her tied to a rope any longer. There were no more rules in her adult life except the ones she set for herself. One would think she left an abusive relationship because she wanted more, but her actions were in the opposite direction. Ijendu was a disaster not only to herself but to her children.

With a bubbly and extroverted personality, Ije as she was called, often times came across as over bearing. It may have been a result of her intelligence which was considered a bit above board and made it difficult to entertain those of lower thought. It may also have been the result of experiences which had dealt her heavy blows. All through her story, she took steps that were irrational. She surprised herself the most!

On the pages of their stories are little leaven that leaven the lump in the lives of many women who escape bad marital relationships. The experiences leave little to be desired of them. They are sometimes battered beyond recognition; most unfortunate is how unaware they are of their state. Sustaining a relationship is nigh impossible, everyone is a suspect, what then is life?

A journey filled with scars was interrupted by a young doctor's rejection and simple advice. Ije began a search for validation. This was the search she was on all along but knew it not. What did her journey yield? How long did it take? Did the tides turn in her favour? How did she sail with the torrents of life? Was she susceptible to the vagaries of the elements?

Read on!

ℓ

THE VOICE

"IJENDU, JUMP, JUMP, I SAID JUMP. GOD WILL catch you with his outstretched arms," screamed the voice from the other end of the cell phone. As she continued, I imagined myself at a cliff edge facing blue waters. My body took the position of an athlete responding to the 'on your marks' line-up of a referee. "Jump …" she yelled yet again, but before she could end her statement, I found myself up in the air.

The tone was emphatic. The words were uttered one at a time. Each word, very clear. She must have pictured me right in front of her as she expressed her thoughts. I believed this was the last counsel from her. She hung up right after, with a finality that made me flinch. She was unlikely to call me all the way from the United Kingdom again to discuss anything other than progress from my current position.

It was a swift jump, I was temporarily lost, she hung up before I knew it. "Jump? From where? To where? How? When? Just like that?" I did not stop mussing. I had just hung the clothes on the line downstairs when the call came. I stood still for a while wondering my fate. For a moment, 'jump' sounded like suicide. "But how could I possibly jump; did she want me to die?" I queried no one in particular. "What a height to jump from!" I thought. I picked up the bucket and the remaining pegs and made my way inside the house. The rest of the day was slow and empty. I did not know when the sun slunk away, like a cat that had offended its owner and didn't want to be seen at the crime scene, giving the moon the cue to appear. I do not recall being busy, or maybe I was busy, but not in a productive way.

"Jump, Ijendu, jump!" I heard these words again. I turned my neck to the left and then to the right as if to see if the owner of the voice would appear. But there was no one. "Jump, Ijendu jump!" this time, the voice seemed firmer and more serious. Ï won't jump. I can't jump. How can I jump? From where would I jump? This is a tall order!" I retorted. "You can't just tell me to jump, what if I fall? It's not just me, there are children. Where do I begin? How do I hold their hands and perform this feat? Jump? This is suicide, if we escape death, we will be badly injured, broken bones, to say the least.

I won't! I can't! No way, not me! Sleep gently swaddled me, knocking me out once my head hit the pillow. I found myself gliding in a void, with my hands reaching to grab hold of nothing in particular, then going into free fall, as if I was on a roller coaster, moving up with lightning speed, and shooting downwards into some kind of labyrinth, leaving me totally powerless, and then my eyes opened, and it was morning. I did not want to wake up. A fire was burning in me. I was completely disoriented. "Jump, Ijendu, jump!" I heard the voice again. This is tormenting. How can you be this nerve-wracking? Why are you so inconsiderate? Where do you want me to start from? Jump is so easy to say, how about lifting me up and pushing me, or better still jump with me?" I really did not care to whom I was talking. I was by myself in the room. "I'm not jumping nowhere and you had better give it up and stop buzzing in my head!" I found strength to get off the bed and went to the kitchen. Besides making breakfast, I had to prepare the kids for school, and also packed lunches for break time. It was about five in the morning. This was one of my best moments of the day. I was awake and alert. My head was clear and often ready for the day by this time. It was both a reflective and demanding morning. Usually, breakfast was any cereal at home. It did not take much time to prepare and gulp down. Lunch took much longer.

"What does she even mean by jump?" I wondered aloud. "Mummy, are you talking to me?" interrupted my nine-year old daughter. Nena is an early riser. I consider her very independent unlike her brother who will not as much as wear his briefs properly without being compelled.

"What are you doing in the kitchen this early, have you showered?" I asked

"You've been murmuring, I barely heard you. I thought you were singing so I came a bit closer to find out what's going on. I really don't understand you, you've been a bit strange since yesterday mum" she replied.

"Hmmmm, I'm sorry my child, sometimes, being an adult, a responsible adult at that, is a tough job"

"What do you mean, mum?"

"It's nothing for you to worry about. It's part of the difficulty of being an adult, just go and get ready for school. Wake your brother up too."

"Mummmmmmeeee ..." she rubbed both eyes and dropped her voice while turning her head to my face.

"My baby girl, it's a quarter to six, you guys will be late if we continue this conversation now. I will take care of myself. I'm your mum. Get going, get ready for school ok" I ended the discussion.

I hoped I had made the necessary impact. I doubted it though! What was most important was for them to get to school while I continued with my voice war. I knew I was in trouble. This voice was bent on hounding me. I had to quickly get through getting them set for school even though this was part of my favourite mummy duties. Besides the beautiful stories and talks we shared on the way to school, I find the quiet drive back revitalizing. Being alone in the car was a safe zone. It was my personal space. No one eavesdropped or barged into this space. I wound up the windows, turned on the air conditioning, and played soft music in the background. I drove gently as I listened to my inner voice.

"Jumping may be a good idea, you know. What do you have left? If you choose to jump, you will jump really far. You are light. All you need is to close your eyes and take a leap of faith. It's one leap, just one leap."

"What if I miss it?"

"What if you make it? Taking the chance will surely lead to a place you've never been, and perhaps help you get your bearings. It all depends on how you land. A good landing could provide the impetus to do something audacious, but a bad one might cause you to retreat into your shell! A bit like a tortoise facing extinction from a meat-eating predator. Take a chance, just try."

"Noooooo" I shook my head violently and bounced back to reality. The drive home continued quietly and silently. Only the hum from the car stereo gave any indication of life in the car. The fifteen-minute drive seemed like eternity until I finally got to my house. The moment I sighted the black gate, I became doleful, tears streamed down my eyes as I honked for the gate to be opened. The security guard whose job it was to open the gate probably noticed my dismal state. I did not respond to his usual 'I'm sorry madam' whenever he delayed opening the gate by seconds.

"I'm sorry madam, I was in the toilet" he came closer and said. My face was frigid, totally unresponsive. Okon would have known this was not his madam's usual manner. I was a happy and expressive fellow. I never ignored his greetings. I made it my duty to keep him happy so that he would discharge his duties well. Okon was by my door by the time I parked the car. Completing the routine of turning off the ignition, removing the car key, taking my purse, making final checks before getting out of the car, Okon was speaking in his strong eastern accent…

"Madam, I hope everything is okay"

"Yes, Okon, all is well"

"What about Oga, I have not seen him in days, is he okay?"

"Yes, he is, he will soon be back" I lied

"The children, did anything happen?"

"Okon, since when did you start interrogating your madam?" I asked with a stern face

"I'm sorry madam, it's just that you are crying. I hope all is well. I have never seen you cry."

"I'm well, I am well …" I barely finished this sentence before I burst out. I quickly ran to the entrance of the house. Okon must have been confused. He knows I was always full of life. We often cracked jokes and bantered. Okon was more of a brother than a servant. With me, everyone was equal, a common zest for the good life, love, pain, and the multifarious duties fate and our metabolisms demand of us, are the common denominators. No one should be lord over the other. This was my belief. I did not know how to be the typical 'oga madam', a phrase used to describe the master's wife during the colonial days. This attitude stuck with many women especially those who married rich men. I did not marry a rich man. We grew our wealth. It took hard work, commitment, diligence and focus on our part. Charles and I contributed a hundred percent each to get to our present state. This is my modest way of inferring how hard I worked, juggling motherly duties and making money. I sat down in the living room and wept my heart out.

"Ijendu, jump, jump, God will catch you" the voice echoed an umpteenth time.

"I can't jump! I won't jump! I don't know how to jump. Where do I jump from and where do I jump to?" My head was between my sweaty palms covering my ears, with eyes shut, nose dripping, and lips that quivered. I slumped to my knees, face down, in praying mode.

"Stop telling me to jump Ifeoma, stop it, stop it. I won't jump. I am married to stay. I married for life. I will make it work. I shall die in it. It's for better for worse till death do us part. My mother did not leave her husband, my sister did not either. There is no one in my family I know that did. Ifeoma, stop, shut your mouth and stop. I will not leave this man. I will not leave this house. This is my house. This is my sweat. Shall I leave all these for another woman? Oh no! Will my children grow up against the backdrop of a broken home? Ifeoma, stop, stop this advice. It's from the pit of hell. I am a Christian woman. This storm will pass, he will get over this stage, and we will overcome. I won't jump" I heaved a sigh of relief feeling like a champion who had just surmounted a Goliath. I was drenched in sweat. The room felt hot even with the air conditioner on. I gently made for the closest sofa and sat, leaning my head backwards, and stretched out my legs, crossed my arms over my chest and drifted into a deep thought.

It was the fifth day of April, 2006; Charles was due to go on a business trip out of the country. I saw him to the airport. I drove home in my van, fully resolved that Charles would not return to the house. I was going to move all our things to the new house he just paid for. He did not think I could pull it off. He asked that I wait until he returned in a week's time. The 'good wife' in me would not let my darling husband down. I needed to prove my dependability. I'm a stallion, at least I thought I was. I worked hard for my family. I pleased my man by making our home comfortable at all times. His duty was to bring home more money, mine was to serve him and the children with all my means. Keeping the home was my strong point.

As soon as I got home from the airport, I started packing. One by one the items in the living room got put into cartons and sacks and finally in to my car. I drove them to the new house, unpacked and arranged them with the help of Okon and some boys who hung around the house. In three days, I had moved everything. I had unpacked, repacked and organised the house. The house swallowed every belonging we had. It was a bigger house. I felt great! This was the beginning of a happier life for our small family. Little by little, piece after piece, I began to fill this new house. I filled it not just with household items, but with love and warmth. Day by day, we grew, all of us. We grew in love, in wisdom and in grace. Our home looked perfect. The family picture on the wall summarized it. It had the four of us with smiles, the genuine smiles of happy people. Charles looked every inch the man of the house. In between, were the children. Ide sat next to me while Nena was beside her dad. This was our first and only family portrait.

There was a problem. This house that I thought I was filling was infact leaking, and I knew it not! My labour, my self-absorption, my work ... "Jump, Ijendu, jump" the voice came again. I jumped to my feet like a wounded lion and raced to my room. This voice is callous. It would not even allow me savour the sweet memories. "Ifeoma must be a witch. How can she continuously echo in my head after this much resistance? I could not possibly be imagining it, could I?" It is possible I had watched too many Nigeria movies! A lot of Nigerian movies depicted voodoo as a powerful religion. They flaunted wizardry of all sorts with effortless maneuverability. Some of them were really amusing and unimaginable. I considered quite a lot of them as great creative pieces. "If these witches and pastors were this powerful, evil would not have been triumphing over good in our land" I usually reminded myself. With too many such movies airing on the African Magic channel, folks are taunted with the phrase, 'too much Africa magic intake' when they complained of seeing ghosts or being chased at night by some creepy looking creatures. It was common practice here to seek spiritual help for every problem one faced. If a child did not thrive in mathematics, we were quick to pray or visit a priest. For marriage to succeed, a prophetess or an imam had the solution. To get a husband and to flourish in business, we consulted the oracles through a '*dibia*' or an '*ifa*' priest. A woman advanced in age without a husband, prompts her mother to visit a 'seer' on her behalf. To get a male child and to attract great spouses were not exempted either! These are independent of the offerings of our various pastors and church leaders.

Nigerians are supposedly highly spiritual even though I consider this trait a bit stupid. The actions do not tally with our portrayed sophistication. We believe in science. We go to school. We have college education and our children excel globally, yet we are undeniably superstitious, how paradoxical! I was not an exception. Here was I believing Ify's (that's what I called Ifeoma for short) voice was so powerful that it was literally chasing me. "I bind you, stupid voice in Jesus name. I bind you. I resist you. I command you to go back to the pit of hell where you came from." I screamed as I got into my room and continued in tongues for an hour. I spoke in tongues. I was proud to. I used this at every opportunity. How else would the devil fear me? The entire kingdom of hell must know that there was fire in me. Once I faced any difficulty, the first reaction was to speak in tongues accompanied with some acrobatic movement. This was my norm. Anyone who had spent many years in Pentecostal churches like I had, would most likely be like that. We believed in praying without ceasing, praying first and praying last. Praying was the first action to be taken in dire situations. We believed that when we pray, God turned the situation around. There is veracity in this but I have learnt to pray and act simultaneously. Days rolled into weeks. The command from Ifeoma constantly reverberated in my subconscious. I got tired of 'binding and casting' the demonic voice away. Ify did not call me again. She had her challenges; she had a sick son she was attending to. I didn't know how she had time to listen to my woeful tales all the time. I guess she got tired and screamed, "Ijendu, jump, jump, God will catch you" before hanging up the telephone that day. Her voice haunted me until I made a decision. I was going to jump. I made up my mind that someday I would jump; and then I called Ify.

"Babes, I have given God an ultimatum, if by the last day of July things do not change, I will simply do the needful".

"Look Ijendu, stop giving ultimatums, its two weeks to your so-called ultimatum day, what do you think will be different? If you want to do this, you better do it and when you do, stick to it. Don't raise false alarms. When you raise an alarm, people will come to help you, if it is false, they will eventually disregard your false alarms and you may never win their sympathy again. You better plot your graph and do this once and for all." Ify no longer minced words in talking to me. Her punches were menacing! I was sure she didn't care if she hit below the belt or the chest region. She threw her jabs anywhere and everywhere.

Few years ago, Ify and I had met through a mutual friend. She ran a shop for women's clothes. She was very focused and friendly in her business approach. When I didn't have sufficient funds, she offered me credit while other times, she worked around my budget. She was always calm and encouraging, one would hardly know she had her pile of challenges. She prayed with me and supported me with money. Our relationship grew to the point we were blunt about our analysis of each other's situation. I was proud to call her my friend. I confided in her. We shared our high and low moments together. We were in the same age range, and so were our children.

We faced similar challenges in our homes. We had so many common denominators. When I call Ifeoma my friend, she was indeed my friend. Ify chose to be brutally honest with me this time. "I will send you a friend's number. Call her to connect you with her lawyer. I already spoke to her. Do this and do it fast." She hung up again. A few seconds later she sent Dazie's number.

I called.

"Hello Dazie, my name is Ijendu, Ify gave me your number"

"Oh yeah, she called me. How are you and the children?"

"We are good, thanks and you? Your daughter?" "I have to be in a prayer meeting this evening, I think you should come. We need to pray over this"

"I am done praying please. All I need is your lawyer's contact number"

"I will give you his number but before you call him, I need you to be sure of what you want to do. You need to really pray about this. It's a rough road."

"I have prayed. I am praying and I will keep praying. Please send the number, thank you"

"If you insist, but I wish you would come to our fellowship this evening. We can pray together"

"Can I get the number please?"

"Why not, I will send it. Ify told me you are a good Christian and would have prayed your heart out, but how about we pray over this one more time?"

"You and I will pray, don't worry about it, just give me the number and I will contact you for prayers later please". I was getting irritated at her insistence. Could this be the way I had been making Ify feel? Could this be how foolish I had been 'casting away' Ify's demonic voice? I waited for the contact details. A few minutes later, there was still no message from Dazie, I called Ify, "Babes, *dis your friend own pass me*. I don't understand this insistence to be in her church for more prayers before giving me the lawyer's contact"

"Don't mind her, I told her not to take you through such rigour. She will give it to you, just don't budge. Don't go with her to any church *abeg*" "Alright then, I will wait for her but I will not call her again"

"I'll call her, relax, she will give you the number. Just be sure you are decisive. This will cost you but you have to decide to move forward".

My spine was literally shivering. These prayer lines had suddenly doused my resolve. I started to feel like a sinner headed for hell fire in a customized jet. "God must be disappointed with me" I thought hard. I lost interest in having the contact details. I did not bother anymore. I was not going to call her any longer. And even if she sent it, I would not bother myself contacting the lawyer. I did not want to be a sinner. To think that Dazie recently got divorced amazed me the more at her disposition. One would have thought she would be interested in my predicament and be more empathetic rather than playing a holier-than- thou card. It is often said that you can take a drowning man from the water but you need to also take the water out of him. I was not sure Dazie had got over whatever made her end her relationship. "How could she be so blinded and insensitive?" I had no plans to keep her in my circle, not as a friend, not even an acquaintance. She probably meant well too. Perhaps she was doing all she knew how to do. I always weighed both sides. If she knew better, she would have done things differently. This may also mean that divorce simply ends a physical relationship with a specific individual. The emotional strings may still be unbroken, otherwise, what would have been the prayer topic had I joined her in church?

While I was in contemplation, my phone beeped. It was Barrister Udeme's phone number, Dazie had sent it. After a minute or two, Dazie called to verify that I got the message. "I already called Udeme, he is expecting your call. I think you should call him right away" she said. "Sure, immediately, I replied" I was outside. I learnt to do all my telephone conversations out of earshot of anyone, and if Charles had set up any gadget to monitor me, it would be useless. Most often, I made my private calls when I got to the children's school to pick them up. He could not have set up any monitoring device in their school, since it's not his territory. At home, Okon was at his beck and call and the children were used by him to monitor me too. There was Ngozi his sister who lived with us. I was unable to fathom the joy she derived being his spy. Ngozi was a beautiful young soul. She and Nena had a remarkable semblance. I loved her very much. I took on the role of being her mother. Perhaps I did not play it well or she did not want me to play it at all. Somewhere along the line, we ceased to get along. I was not certain at what point she became a spy for her brother. Other neighbours indiscriminately provided unsolicited information to him too. For the children and the neighbours, I knew they meant no harm but for Ngozi and Okon! They were on his payroll. I could never understand this level of insecurity, distrust or manipulation. It left me confused for many years. I wondered fruitlessly what I must have done to stir such cynicism. The few times I confronted him , he denied it. I could bear the rest but not my children. These were really young innocent minds, to set them to question their mum's every move and inform him was intolerable. I found it insensitive, callous and the height of irresponsibility. I knew I had to be a one-man gang. So many people were watching me and giving information based on their assumptions. I found out that facts were grossly misrepresented, but then, it was too late. My heart ached and still aches.

"Good morning Barrister Udeme, my name is Ijendu. Barrister Dazie recommended you"

"Ok madam, how are you doing? I guess you prefer to come to my office. Do you want to come today or tomorrow?"

"Tomorrow morning sir, after morning school run"

"Okay then, see you there"

"Please can I get the address of your office and will you be there say 8am?"

"It's at Gudu, yes I will be there, No 34 Ado crescent, Gudu, once you are on your way, give me a call. It's by Parliament School"

"Alright sir, see you tomorrow, thank you very much" I hung the phone with a sigh of relief. "The deal was sealed or semi sealed. I will have to jump but maybe not as soon as Ify thinks" I contemplated aloud before driving off for school runs.

Barrister Udeme was hospitable. "Madam, if you are not that buoyant, I'm afraid you may not be able to afford me. How about moving out of the house with the children, face your life. If he likes, he can file for divorce. There is no law that mandates the two of you to live together". "Alright sir, thank you very much" I stood up to leave. "You will be fine, stay strong and remain positive. If there are further issues, don't hesitate to give a call. All the best!" he concluded. I left his office. I had direction. I knew where to start. I got home in one piece. I knew it was just a matter of time; the time was very close. I had lived in denial for so long. What I feared had finally come upon me, I remembered the travail of biblical Job. I braced for the confrontation.

Anticipation of death is worse than death itself they say. I began the process of waiting, the long wait of a life time. I had to have an exit plan. I needed my family. I needed money. I could do with a few friends and perhaps knowledge of the law. The children had to at least complete the term. This was the longest two weeks of my life.

In the days leading up to 21st August of that year, Rotimi visited. Rotimi was Charles' business partner. I knew him but not in-depth. I had worked with Charles for a number of years and I knew all the regular partners who worked closely with him. Rotimi was one of those we secured credit from. When we got a medium or big supply that we were unable to finance, Rotimi offered support, he got paid once we got paid. Rotimi had a small frame, dark skinned and stuttered. He was an active member of his local church and talked about Christ often. He was taken by our work together, in emulation, he brought his wife to head his company's finance and administrative department. We shared a good family relationship on the surface. Seeing him in the house was a sigh of relief. I thought I could trust him. We talked about the tension between Charles and I and how I was not seeing any silver lining. I opened up as much as I could. I felt embarrassed because I had modelled a good wife to all those around us. Talking with him about the issues I had with Charles was both relieving and unburdening. He was surprised to hear of the series of domestic violence. He looked at me in disbelief though. When I mentioned that his friend Charles had not been sleeping in the house for weeks, his mouth was agape. He was much more astonished to learn of the series of infidelities I had caught Charles in. I was not sure I had done the right thing exposing our relationship to his friend. I probably should not have done so. In this clime, men were always right. They supported each other; more so, I did not know Rotimi's agenda! Was he neutral? Was he for me, or against me? Just before he left, the words he uttered seemed to have had an undertone that I was the problem, and I should bear the consequences of whatever happened afterwards. I wasn't sure I'd heard right until a few days later.

After he left, I weighed his words and his body language. I felt unsure, and was even more convinced I'd spoken to the wrong person. I should have been more cautious, but who really remained fully alert in such awkward circumstances? I was emotionally low, very low at that. With Charles, it was both emotional and physical torture. He was a calculative man from my point of view, unlike me and my carefree nature. I was quick to trust and even quicker to forgive.

Rotimi called me on the phone, he recorded our conversation and sent it to Charles. Charles sent it to Nwachi my brother. Nwachi forwarded it to me as evidence and an exhibit that would be tendered in court. The only sentence I found fault with was "if things don't change by August 30th, I will activate my action plan". I was blamed for the threat. While I considered this a time frame for Charles to retrace his steps, another line of thought was that I threatened to kill him. I was pained. I did not know that Rotimi was also part of the plot working against me. The resolve to continue as a one-man army, not trusting anyone any longer, was stronger. I should not have been surprised but for the fact that he professed Christ. He was a counselor in his local church. I know that counselors were discreet, they do not further divide, they sought peace. I remember going through rudiments of counseling in my church. I saw him as an elder in the church of God. Again, I was awakened to the fact that perhaps the bible was not meant to be lived out verbatim. The people here who we looked up to sang different tunes. Their lives differed from their actions. Charles quoted the bible very well. He went to church. His younger brother was a priest of the Roman catholic church. He was raised in a very religious home; his parents were knights and respected elders in their local church. Many times, I saw him twist the contents to suit his game and his whims at any given time. Perhaps, the bible role is to control our lives. I may be wrong. I hope I am.

I'm not sure I fully digested the effect of the backstab from Rotimi. I knew his loyalty was with his friend but then, did he not say he was on a peace mission? I thought a person with such an intention took no sides and didn't get involved in any act that escalated the problem he came to ameliorate. On the one hand, I didn't consider him smarter than me, so how could I have allowed him pull such a silly stunt on me? I now disliked him, everything about him! Rotimi needed to give me a detailed explanation about this else I doubt he would see the God he believes in, after life on earth!

The more I thought about Charles the more livid I became. I was most infuriated by the fact that he didn't look even remotely like the man I was describing. Should Rotimi express this fact in future as the reason for his poor arbitration, I will understand. He probably got fooled like many of us. Again, perhaps I should empty my anger on the society, the society that held a woman solely responsible for the failure of a marriage contract: the society that exalts one human above another simply because that human has a penis. Ours is a society that equates 'male' with 'leader!'.

Weeks became days, days became hours and hours became minutes as the clock ticked... In the early hours of a beautiful Friday morning, we took the big leap of faith.

2

THE BENCHERS

A FEW DAYS AFTER I HAD TAKEN BACK MY LIFE, and still floating in my new reality, I was deep in thought. Despite the waiting, I had no concrete plan on how to forge ahead. I had no job, no friend, no colleague and no neighbour I could count on. I had become very comfortable being a one-man squad. As I reminisced, I realized that it was no longer necessary to be by myself. I needed people. No one should be without money and without people too. As a child, my father taught us that one with people is not a poor man. I reached for my phone and began a search for people who would stick out their necks for me. Two things were on my mind, delete the useless names and reach out to possible helpers. I scrolled through more than a hundred names on my phone. "Surely, one of these should be helpful" I thought as I scrolled on. One by one, I reflected on each contact's usefulness. It was a necessary phone clean up. Anyone who posed a threat was taken off. Those who supported Charles were not just deleted but also blocked. It was an emotional but meticulous exercise; there were some names I did not imagine I would delete. I felt they had betrayed me. I had had high expectations of them but they had let me down. My face was drawn, but I still managed to be attentive until I saw Barrister Essien's name. I smiled. He could be my saviour!

Barrister Essien's children attended the same school as my children and I was an administrator there. He introduced himself to me as a lawyer. To me, he dressed too stylishly for a lawyer. He wore mostly white and blue shirts over black trousers, as if trying to press onlookers about his style and class. He was about five foot ten inches. He was fair complexioned, talked authoritatively and seemed unfriendly. Our paths crossed daily when he came for pick-ups, and from the way he ogled me, I sensed he had an interest in me. I will not forget the day he asked for my number. He was faster than lightening.

"You have my number, right? Please call me, call me today" he asked hurriedly ......

"Yes, I do" I answered.

He was gone before I could complete my response. I had access to all parents', staff and vendors details considering my position. His request did not sit well so I paid deaf ears to it. The next day, he asked why I did not call and requested for the direct school line to my office. I obliged him. He called. He was humorous and pleasant. He nicely asked for my personal line. I knew he was being friendly; I kept an open mind.

Barrister Essien called a few times, not surprisingly, but he showed his hand too early when he offered me an unsolicited all expenses paid trip to London, plus every other thing under the sun if I became his. But this was the thing with the Nigerian man who felt entitled to a trophy as soon as he has a little "change" in his pocket, then a woman naturally kowtowed to his corrosive demands.

"Have you forgotten I'm married?" I asked

"I'm married too" he replied.

"Then go and face your wife" I chided.

"Are you not a woman? You will succumb one day. You will be mine, let's bet"

"God forbid! Not in my life. I shall never dishonour my husband, my king, not in my life"

"Leave that thing, just relax for me baby" he said with an air of arrogance.

"Please don't ever call me again. I'm married, show some respect and leave me in peace!" I hung up.

Our last encounter on the phone was not very pleasant. It was either I had punctured his pride or he was re-thinking his strategy. I was grateful for whatever reason he had to bother me no more. He never took it out on me in anyway. Our relationship remained professional, he was a parent and I was a staff for the duration of my stay.

I held my phone, stared at his name as I recollected. "So where is the marriage you were protecting?" I asked myself rhetorically. "If you were circumspect, you would have used the opportunity wisely" the critical inner voice continued. "I did what I had to do. And I do not regret it" the voice reacted defensively. I dropped the phone gently on the bed and began to think of what to do with his name. Was I to delete, block or make contact? If I called, what would I say? What if he gave me a taste of my medicine? The reason for going through my phone was to activate a support system. I needed to reach out to friends. I knew there would be a battle. Charles would fight back. We had separated; we were not divorced yet. He would fight for custody. He would want a proper divorce. He already had a lover and may be interested in tying the knot with her. Again, I had no job, no house, no money. A support system was vital and inevitable. Barrister Udeme told me I could not afford his services. Indeed, Dazie confirmed he was thorough but way out of my league, money- wise. In my immediate circle, I had no friend who was a lawyer. I gave everything to Charles and the children. I disconnected from friends and family; this position became regrettable. Nigerians are wise. We made friends in every sphere. There was an unwritten code of 'knowing who knows who' that most of us operated with. I ignored this code. I was immersed in my little world, how foolish! My options as far as legal representation was concerned, were limited, Essien was an option to try. I had no alternative."

"Good evening sir, my name is Ijendu from Yorkshire Basic School. I hope you remember me. I have a very personal issue I would like to discuss privately with you. Would it be in order if I requested an appointment?"

The nicely crafted short message was all I could summon. I was swift to send it. One very good thing about mobile phone technology was the chance to be dispassionate and yet communicate, and quite quickly too. The time was 9:47pm. I waited for a response until I slept off. I had a peaceful sleep; the best of the last few weeks. The next day started slowly. I was reluctant to open my eyes and get out of bed. I was not going to work anyway, there was no job to rush to. As I bided my time, imagining what the day would look like, I remembered my unfinished business. I took my phone and saw his response – "if it's you, call me in the morning". I checked the time, it was 8:18am. I figured that it was a good time so I called.

"Hello sir, this is Ijendu from Yorkshire School"

"Good morning, and what in the world would make you call me this early today?"

"It is about my marriage, it has crashed and I need your assistance," I blurted.

"I'm so sorry to hear about your marriage. What happened? How long ago was this? Do you have a lawyer? You know I'm a lawyer, right?"

With one hand holding the phone by my ear, the fingers of the other hand taking turns between my teeth, I was nodding my head as if he was standing with me. I was as nervous as could be. "Are you there?" he questioned

"Yes sir, I am"

"Can you come to my office if you are not too busy?"

"What time would you want me come?"

"I'm not so busy now, you can come right away. Do you have a car? Anyway, you can take a taxi, I will pay."

I considered myself underserving of this kind gesture. I took this invitation with much seriousness. I followed his description until I got to the gate of his big house. For a moment, I thought I was a panjandrum considering the manner his security ushered me in. I was pleased and honoured. I was also humbled. We were by no means in the same class. Standing there, I knew I was unqualified to be his client. If Barrister Udeme's fees were immodest, his would be worth a king's ransom! I followed the directions to the entrance, just before I knocked, the door opened. Essien gave me a warm welcome with a smile and motioned for me to come in. The first room I stood in was fascinating. The flower vase and the paintings on the wall were simple, but looked rich. The fragrance was floral. I was intimidated. My legs became numb as I considered the magnificence of the house.

"Welcome to our humble abode" he said

"Thank you, thank you, thank you" I replied

"Please come along" he continued

"Thank you" I responded

We walked through a short aisle into a living area.

"This is where I receive visitors like you, please have a seat and be comfortable. I will be with you shortly" he said as he took a dash.

"Thank you"

I made up my mind to be on my best behaviour being as this was my first time in such a rich environ as this. I sat upright with my chest out on a cute red sofa, my legs crossed in a royal manner. There were pictures of his wife and children hanging on the wall. The room was tastefully fitted out. "Could this be his office?" I asked myself. In a few minutes, he joined me. He was simply dressed in a striped shirt tucked into a pair of navy-blue trousers. His black shoes were glittering, I could see my face in them. I looked at his waist and was not disappointed by his belt. Essien was a man of class! Everything I saw was in tandem with his persona.

"Am I that special?" I inquired

"What do you mean?"

"You said you received visitors like me here"

"You don't like it? You want to go to the inner chambers?"

"Oh!" Is that what you meant?"

"Acquaintances, first time clients, unfamiliar people do not go beyond this point. We discuss whatever brings them and then they leave. This is a very big house, you could get lost in here. I hope I did not offend you"

"Not in the least, I needed clarification"

"You are too academic! You are untying a simple sentence? Anyway, welcome. Would you like anything before I take you round?"

"I'm fine, thank you"

"Not even a glass of juice?"

"I'm alright sir, thank you"

"Let me show you round then. Come with me"

I followed. I was thoroughly impressed. His house was fit for kings only.

He used another wing of his tastefully furnished house as an office. This was where we ended up. His desk, shelves, chandelier, settings and all that fitted into his office space were beautifully put together. I considered him a man of simple and exquisite taste. I was loving what I saw and the ambience around him.

"I did not know you were a politician, when do you have time for law practice?"

"Law is my occupation, politics is my vocation" he said. I reminded myself to quickly focus on the business of the day. Whatever he meant by his last statement did not make sense in anyway. I usually do not let such talk slide past me. I would have taken him on but I restrained myself. He is not just a lawyer but a Nigerian politician. I became wary of him. I hoped that my journey would not be futile. Politicians in our clime are masters at double speak. They know how to launch a rocket from their living rooms.

They can build roads in the air and get water from the rocks. To me, Nigerian politicians are exceptional with their gift of the gab. This was my very first personal encounter with one. He was a top politician, very powerful in his state.

"To what did I owe this nicety?" I could not help but reason aloud.

"You deserve it, you sure deserve it, please sit and feel at home," he replied. "I'm sorry to hear about your marriage. Would you like to tell me the details or should we go straight to why you wanted to see me?" he spoke sitting across his posh desk. I was bereft of speech as I admired his office setting. I was more relaxed in his office than the main house. I took many glances at the framed pictures of his family. They seemed happy and well cared for. His wife was beautiful. I had seen her a few times at the school. The pictures portrayed a perfect family. I was jealous. Everything – his house, cars, photographs and behaviour, coupled with the ambience of the scenery added up except that I did not understand what he wanted in another woman.

Having realized he was a politician; I was skeptical about proceeding with any discussion. "I came because you are a lawyer. I know I cannot afford you, perhaps you can help in some way. I'm not only out of cash, because I do not have a job presently. It's quite tough but I will pull through. How can you be of help to me, please?" I could not look at him in the face. I recalled with shame how sternly I treated his offer of an amorous relationship. My short sightedness had not the faintest idea that tables could turn hence I did not apply any sort of diplomacy. With my bent head, I was imagining the worst and was ready for whatever answer he gave.

"Well, I'm an apostle of divorce. This is my second marriage. If it's not working, you should pack it in. I hope there was no physical violence?"

"There was, simply put. I survived, but I'm not so sure I want to go into details. I wish to know what you can do for me."

"Should it not be the other way round? You sought me, what do you want, legal justice or jungle justice?"

"Jungle justice? How do we give jungle justice in marital cases?"

"Jungle justice has only one meaning, do you want it?"

My mind took a quick dash down memory lane. A picture of a dark, slim young male adult caught by an angry mob for allegedly stealing a phone became vivid. He was wailing and begging for his life. "Please, don't kill me" he pleaded with his two hands together. His face was muffled up in blood, tears, sweat and sand. The angry mob had beaten him thoroughly. He was unrecognizable, with his shredded clothes and battered body. His voice was faint, a sign of tiredness from crying. A tyre was hung over his neck and in a flash, he was set ablaze as soon as someone emptied a bottle of fuel over his head. I stood still for a while, took a deep breath then shook my head vehemently.

"Nooooooo," I screamed.

"Why not?" he asked.

"Does it mean killing or just beating him?"

"Make your choice."

"And what about legal justice?"

"Well, we can simply ruffle him a bit, get you an *Oluwole* divorce certificate. You can carry on with your life. Legal justice is exhausting. The process is rather long. We may not have the patience." He further expatiated on both. His explanations were insightful. Without a doubt, I was floating in oblivion in this area.

"Let me know your decision asap" Barrister Essien interrupted my thought.

"I don't want him ruffled please. Leave him with God."

"You are so naïve! How do you leave a man that so manhandled you with God? Are you sure you told me the truth? Were you faithful, tell me, did he catch you with another man?"

"Never! Not me. The thought never crossed my mind"

"If you choose litigation, I usually like to handle cases that give me lots of money. I am a busy man as you can see. However, I can give your case to my boys."

"What will it take? I mean the figures …"

"I guess you can pay per appearance, it should not be more than ten thousand naira. I will recommend the other option though. It will cost you nothing. I will simply use my political machinery. Let me order breakfast for you. Make yourself comfortable, use the other chair please."

I moved to the other side of his office and sat on the sofa. Anyone looking could see confusion all over me. I had to quickly make a decision, one was at no cost, swift, with justice assured, while the other would not only cost me, it would also waste my time. I was taken aback by his courtesy and professionalism. I expected some bashing and tongue lashing. So far, he had treated me well. I was confused the more. The idea of jungle justice had never surfaced in my calculations. This would have given me some satisfaction but for the uncertainty of living. He may die. He may get deformed. I did not want any regrettable outcome, Charles remained the father of my children, harming him was not an option, in the real sense, I had no alternative. I was hoping for a pro-bono case from my learned admirer. A wry smile on the corner of his mouth seemingly gave him away and his real intentions showed forth. "I thought you would handle this matter or at best, give me some professional counsel but …"

"What but? You want me to do a case that will fetch me nothing? What is in this for me? Please don't remind me of how you tossed away my friendship and love for this marriage. I won't forget, never!"

Essien was calm all through. He sipped a glass of wine as he spoke to me. What was I expecting in the first place? We were back where we left off.

"Let me take care of you Ije. I will rent a house for you and buy you a car. What do you have to lose? I love you, I really do". I had promised myself to stay focused and I had no plans to renege. I was not going to trust his empty words. Love indeed, I sneered at him in my heart. "I need to leave sir. Let me think about it and I will get back to you, thank you very much." I stood up and headed for the door. "Hold on, have this, you said you didn't have transport fare, right? Let me know your decision as soon as possible." I was quick to take the money offer; how did he know I needed money so badly? I was more than grateful when I counted it and it was fifty thousand naira. This amount was like five million naira. "If you are not in a hurry, I can drop you off. You should probably have lunch before heading home."

"I'm fine, you already gave me breakfast, no need for lunch please."

"Wait! Why are you always stubborn? I want you, you want my help, how about relaxing a bit? How about trading, don't be too hard on yourself. Let me be your man, be my girl. I will sort out things for you. Charles is too small to stop you if you are with a man like me, trust me on this please." He persisted.

I gave up. He took me home; I took some change of clothes and a few personal things. Our first night in the hotel was memorable.

He was in a hurry to inspect his newly acquired 'property'; his hands were all over me as we sat on the bed in the hotel room.

"You can stay till the weekend, it's on me" he said

"Ok" I showed no excitement

"A shower or a drink"

"Both"

He picked up the telephone by the bedside, requested for a drink, an alcoholic drink. I heard him ask for two bottles of a strong wine that I knew. I smiled from where I was changing.

"Here, I got you a night gown" he tossed a bag at me

I scrambled for the bag, opened it …

"Excuse me" I left for the bathroom.

It was such a sexy lingerie! "This man was ready for the kill tonight" I muttered to myself not sure I was on the same plane with his desires. I could imagine the state of his mind! He always wanted an amorous relationship with me. He made frantic efforts some years ago, he offered me an all expense paid trip to any country I chose. "I must be gold and knew it not" I thought to myself. I was almost certain that except with the help of alcohol, it was going to be a disastrous night for him.

"Are you trying out the gown?" he asked a bit loudly "I hope you like it. It was a bit pricey from Abman stores" he continued. Abman stores was reputed for selling expensive ladies lingerie in the city. I smiled at hearing Abman. Finally, I was going to wear lingerie from that store! I saw the price tag; my eyes almost popped out of their sockets.

"My goodness! This money would have done me a lot of good" I shouted.

"Come out, let me see you, the drinks are here too"

"You are definitely not in a hurry, are you? The night is still young" I responded.

It was lacy, silky and white with frills. I judged his taste exquisite once again. With the perfume on me, I was perhaps ready for the night. I stepped into the room beaming from ear to ear. He smiled back at me as if he had done a great job. Indeed, he had set the tone. The light was off but for the illumination from the television. It was an average sized room, well fitted and inviting. Surprising his clothes were still on; he was sipping the red wine he ordered. I was not to be a kill joy …

I sat on the one-seater sofa, with my drink in my hand wondering who would make the first move. The stage was apparently set for him, for us, but this was his script. My long legs were crossed, a glass of red wine in my hand, for a moment, I was lost in thought.

"Over here baby" he beckoned

I moved straight to the bed into his arms and the kissing game began. It was mechanical. I wasn't tipsy yet. He paused, took off his shirt, then his singlet. He took my hands and placed them on his belt. I helped to pull it off followed by his pants. He was standing, I matched his height as our lips locked with closed eyes for a minute or two. It was a great kiss! I gulped the last of the drink in my glass, he poured more and asked me to gulp, I did, I took another gulp this time lying on the bed. From my neck to the chest his hands were everywhere. "You have a great body, it's ravishing, why have you been hiding it? It doesn't look like you've had children. Everywhere is firm, soft, glowing, let me take care of you baby" his fingers were slowly finding their way everywhere. I was relaxing, the bed was soft, the melodic music from his phone, the drink, his words, everything was in his favour. I had to cooperate. Our eyes met again. "Trust me, you are gold. You are more beautiful than I imagined. I want you, I want you every day. Be mine, please baby, be mine…" I stopped hearing him the moment he latched on one nipple.

He left in the middle of the night. He had a policy of not spending the night outside his home. I respected it. I slept well for the rest of the night, thanks to the alcohol. The minute I woke, my mind began to go wild in thoughts; free legal representation, jungle justice, dating a married man, my children's welfare, a job, a house, my new role as a concubine et al. I hadn't had sex in many years. For me, I have to be involved emotionally to enjoy coitus. I was sure he noticed. He was gentle all through. He tried to carry me along. I was grateful that he bore with my lack of participation that one night. Months went by, we became a pair, secret lovers. Essien had a great family. He talked about his wife and how awesome she was as a wife. According to him, his heart was drawn to me hence he was keen to have me. He professed love and could not understand why he loved his wife and I with the same intensity. He always begged me to remain with him. He wanted to have a baby with me as sign of his love. All that he offered looked juicy, very intriguing and appealing. I was in between the devil and the deep blue sea. He looked rich no doubt, but he was no longer in government. The politicians in power doled out monies to their concubines in millions and not in thousands. He was still using cheap hotels and giving me small monies. Besides not being ready for another committed relationship, I doubted his ability to live up to his word. He couldn't even give me one of his cars. He wouldn't rent a house for me until I got pregnant. We continued our foolery, to me, we were both having a ride, a foolish ride at that. All seemed cool between us until I got the divorce summon from Charles. Essien suddenly became unwilling to help. He was full of excuses. He discouraged me from legal proceedings, advocated for an out of court settlement and hyped jungle justice. From the few months we had spent together, I noticed that money was not flowing as I heard of politicians and their girlfriends. He kept asking me to be patient with him when I brought up his promises of a nicer apartment and a car. All the promises before we kicked off became like the campaign promises of a Nigerian politician. I was livid because I had gone all the way with him in exchange for free litigation and all other benefits. I should have remembered he rooted for jungle justice. I had to look for Barrister Udeme.

At Barrister Udeme's office, he handed me over to his staff Itua. Itua looked young and sharp. While taking my brief, he interrupted me a few times with ''you are so beautiful'. I was observing. This really was my first business dealing with lawyers. I could understand Essien but Itua was confusing.

"You will pay 5k per representation." He said.

"Five thousand? I asked

"Yes, is there any problem?"

"Not at all, thank you"

"Five thousand naira was cheaper than my previous offer of ten thousand naira" I thought in my mind. He did some necessary documentations before we bade each other bye. In between the few times Itua appeared in court to defend me, he asked me for sex. He said he was greatly attracted to me.

"Just once madam and I will never have to ask again" he entreated. I detested him in my mind. On a good day, I would never have listened to him. He was not just younger but thin. There was nothing comely about him. He was neither rich nor handsome. I'm not sure his intelligence was anything out of this world. He was married. Thinking about him got me very infuriated. How does he have the temerity to utter such a proposal? I was miffed.

"Look, you'd better stay in your lane and don't ever think of me in that light again. Do I look so loose to you? Is this how you work?"

"I'm sorry madam. It's just that I cannot resist you. Just look at your hips, even your skin kills me." He was supposed to be apologizing. I hung the phone. He resorted to sending messages to my phone.

Itua would start with professional jargon and infuse his inordinate desires and continue with more information. I was not sure what reporting him to his principal would yield. I could excuse Essien, he wanted me from the word go but this stupid Itua had no excuse. As I contemplated, I got a message on my phone;

'you don't have to be so hard. I admire you, we are both adults, we can please ourselves and there is no big deal about it. Your case comes up in two days, please remember to keep me in your budget'.

"Idiot!" I mussed. Just then, Nafisat's call came through.

Nafisat was in my exact situation, younger by a few years, dark and beautiful. Her hubby left her for another woman. He did not just leave, he converted to Islam to please his new wife. Nafisat's story seemed more compelling than mine. I met her in a Facebook group for women. We were quick to connect. We squeezed time to see each other and stayed happy. Each time she recounted any part of her story, she did so in tears. I cried with her, encouraged her as much as I could. She had no job at the time, her family supported her with feeding while her ex-husband paid the children's school fees. Her appearance gave no inclinations to what she was suffering. She was chubby and classy. She drove a good car. Kindo, her ex-husband was comfortable and good looking. He had a few properties all over the city, serving as the chief executive officer of his logistics company. There were two lovely girls between them. They went to church together, and were always 'the couple' until 'Kindo started being physically violent. His anger was ignited by anything. He was that spontaneous and dangerous. "When he got inflamed, he used anything within reach, knife, shoe, belt, bottle … I don't know how I escaped alive" Nafisat recalled with teary eyes. "I enjoyed his money. He was very rich but all that is gone at the moment". She continued. Nafisat was struggling to find her feet. At the time we met, she was trying her selling skills with fashion accessories. The trunk of her car was her stall. Once she dropped the children in school, she went from home to home, office to office, shop to shop scouting for customers. She was very determined. Kindo had no plans for her in his wealth. Just like Charles, Kindo's position was to have custody and if Hafisat insisted, then he would have no hand in their upkeep. The court was yet to finalise their case.

"Hi girlfriend" I answered

"Babe, any groove today? It's Friday"

"I had no plans, I don't even have money and there was no company"

"I'm company enough, we can hang out in my house. I've got some drinks and some snacks. I will call up a few friends if you are up to it."

"I'm game, expect me about 7pm"

"Cool, see you then"

Our conversation was brief. I would have to seek her opinion on Itua. A few ladies who had broken marriages threw caution to the wind and pleased their bodies indiscriminately. I was wondering if rejecting Itua would affect his performance on my case. Sometimes, I gave some thought to making him a toy in my pocket despite being completely unattractive to me; after all, this was how men treated women. From my interaction with Nafisat, she was no longer the comely girl next door. She used marijuana, drank a lot of alcohol and hung around bad boys. We had a party in her house once where she made food with marijuana and served. I recall drinking 'zobo', a locally made russell drink and was surprised to have gotten dizzy. She confessed to having laced all the drinks and food with drugs! She wanted everyone in high spirits so that the party would not be a dull one. Everyone got high, I inclusive. Thankfully, I did not have random sex that night. I was very careful with life. I grew up very religious and as much as I tried, I was trapped in my religious mindset. I hated it as much as I liked it. It kept me from indulging in what I would rather not do, going by the messages I heard in church. The pastor's voice echoes in my ears the moment I make a wrong step. Sometimes, I shrugged it off, other times, I yielded to it. "Flee, flee from every appearance of evil. Flee from premarital sex!" the pastor's voice haunted me incessantly. I hated it because it made me feel out of place, lily-livered, not courageous enough to live the life I fancied. I was in a dilemma between throwing caution to the wind, being a party animal and damning the consequences, or staying good, prim and proper and miss 'the life'. I had just turned forty; I should have lived this kind of life in my younger days. I loved Nafisat for being the kind of girl I would have loved to be. She was younger and bolder. She made the courageous decision to have fun and enjoy her life. I envied her a little.

I recall one of the end-of year parties Nafisat hosted for her friends. There were guys and girls. I was different. I didn't smoke, not even the simplest cigarette. I wasn't flirty and clingy with any of the guys. I didn't drink either. "Why are you here then?" Yetunde asked. Yetunde was a soldier girl. She worked with the army as I learnt.

"Huh?" I asked.

"You are a miss-goodie-two-shoes, what are you doing here, this is a party for bad ass bitches" she continued.

"Let her be" interrupted Sonia. Sonia was my friend. I had my reservations about the party, she persuaded me to attend. Having been at Nafisat's party once, I was a bit skeptical at attending another.

"She is already forty, if she can't fit in, then she should not even start." Yetunde replied her. I felt sorry for myself. Should I have come or not? I was afraid of getting drunk and being messed up. I tried to puff a few times, but choked. I could not finish the brandy in my glass cup. I was different in every way including my dressing. Looking around, I knew I had wasted my younger years. I should have done what most girls did.

That night, after the party, the boys left. Some of the girls decided to sleep over and leave the next morning. It was one hell of a night for me! All six of us were single mothers, married and separated. We decided to take our lives back instead of staying sad and down. I brought up Itua's topic. "Imagine a lawyer mixing pleasure with work" I ended with this line.

Almost simultaneously, the three of them laughed at me jeeringly. I could not believe it.

"What's wrong with his request?" Nafisat asked

"I'm wondering" sighed Yetunde

"Excuse me, is he not supposed to be a professional? Why ask his client for sex?" I muttered

"You see what I said, this girl should not be here. She thinks sex is a big deal. Give him sex, he does your case. Finish. Is this a topic?" It seemed Yetunde was getting tired of me.

"Did you do the same with your lawyer?" I asked her.

Of course, not just my lawyer, it's a given with any of these men, you should know. Did you do university in Nigeria at all?" she fired back.

"I slept with my lawyer, there's nothing in it. Sometimes I did not have money to pay him, he took it in kind" Nafisat added.

"Me too. In fact, mine wanted me to be his secret mistress. At a point, he even asked for marriage. I'm not sure it's a big deal. Try it, you may even like it. He may be good at it" Sonia chipped in quietly.

"But, how can …"

"How can what? Ijendu you are always academic. I wonder why you are not a lawyer" Yetunde cut in.

"Don't mind her, she argues over everything, something as simple as sex is a problem for her. Can you pay him? If you can, then pay him. He is even nice; he is asking for sex. For some, you would have been the one begging them to have you at their convenience" Nafisat concluded. I joined in the drinking, trying to wrap my head around their highly explosive jibes.

As the night progressed, we retired to a room. It was a big room with a big bed. All the girls agreed that there was no need of splitting. We were to sleep in one room. Nafisat got another mattress and laid it on the floor. Four of us were on the bed while she was on the floor with one person. We continued conversing until Nafisat interrupted.

"Here are toys, if you want to help yourself, please do". She dropped three dildos on the bed. I was already a bit cold going by Yetunde's remarks on me. The girls scrambled for the toys. Both the conversation and mood changed immediately. We had changed into our sleep wears. I did not plan to sleep over hence I had no sleep wear. At home, I usually slept naked and being all girls, I did not mind. I was naked under the duvet. Yetunde was next to me. She began to touch me. I responded, contrary to her expectations. I touched her; I fondled her breast. She looked at me with some degree of surprise. I gave her a sexy look as if to say I wasn't as timid as she thought. I made for her lips, ran my fingers through them before kissing them. "You are good" she said. I smiled and went to her neck; we flipped our position. I had her under. I took charge of the game. I knew the game; I had watched enough of it on the internet and had had some practices some years ago. To me, the female body is easier to get by with, it's soft with many tickle spots. Her breasts were 'portable' perfect for my cupped hands. I fondled them in various ways. Her face gave away her ecstatic mood. "Don't stop" she moaned. I wanted her to take back her impression of me. The fact that I didn't smoke or drink spirits did not mean I wasn't good in some areas. I ate her up, every bit of her. Soon, everyone was on everyone. It was my first time of having an all girls' binge. I tried to let loose. I really tried especially with sex. I remember Yetunde telling me that I was good with fondling her breasts. What a night!

So, this was it. Lawyers took advantages of us. Did this only happen with abused women, or was it the norm in the legal industry? I hoped not! I was getting ready for a second degree in law. With this attitude, I may have a rethink. They traded their services. Ladies were toys in the hands of male lawyers. "Was this only peculiar to divorce cases or was it the with any case where a lady is unable to pay legal fees?" I wondered to myself. I was among five other ladies, none of them frowned at Itua's behaviour, not one. Indeed, all of them gave in to their lawyers. "I seduced mine" said Gloria. "I lured him to my house since he was being stubborn, he could not resist me. My case was smooth and I got most of my prayers. I would have fucked the judge if I needed to anyway". I recalled Gloria's soft voice as she contributed to the discussion. Hadiza hardly spoke but she did not object either. I learnt she was a smooth operator and unmarried. She had three kids for different men.

As I reminisced on the night, I knew I was in another world and I was unprepared for it. I was going to learn and fast too. Itua was not my kind of guy in any way. His shoes and clothes oozed of poverty; he was smallish, very thin. His face was ugly and his disposition was ungainly. I wondered how he had the guts to even ask for sex from me. Perhaps his confidence came from being a lawyer. I could afford his appearance pay, I could, but I worry he may not give his best if I continued resisting. "Was this how all male lawyers were?" I had never dealt with any before. My mind was hovering. "Did they play gods? They were lawyers, learned folk for goodness sake". I was irritated as I pondered on all that was said that night. None of the ladies had a conclusive case yet. How would they not keep giving in to the randy demands of their lawyers in return for legal representation? I will not sleep with

Itua. Not in my life, I promised myself. I was going to work hard to pay him and if it gets so bad, I would involve his principal but that is if his principal was innocent. With this resolve, I gave in to sleep.

I woke up with a pouncing head ache. I must have had a little too much last night. I had to drive home. We all had to disperse. Everyone was grateful for an amazing night. "These girls are rather wild" I thought. "I wished I lived like this earlier. At forty, I was not sure how much change I could do to my lifestyle. I think Itua's case was a matter of perspective. I could give it a try. He probably will make a good sex toy, no emotions, just a service man. I thought about calling and having him come for a scrutiny test…" I learnt about 'scrutiny test' from Hadiza. She suggested that I invited him over and ensure his tool was worth the risk. If he was, I should carry on but if he wasn't, I should make a big deal of it and he would stop pestering me. I was reneging on my resolution, smiling, reminiscing as I cruised home.

Two weeks later, I met Omoni. She had recently left her marriage due to severe physical abuse. We had not seen in a long while and I was impressed with her looks. She seemed emotionally stable; like one who had got her groove back. I asked after her overall wellness and we agreed to meet up in my home. She kept her word, and visited. We talked about everything, from child bearing to career to dating and sex. We were that open. Then I asked her how she handled legal fees. She was not different. She was the fifth single mum who towed the same line. She paid her lawyer part of his fees and the rest was written off after good sex sessions. I was in shock! She went further to tell me how her friends did the same. "Ada my friend who introduced me to the lawyer gave me the idea. She said that was how she scaled through. In fact, she did not even pay a dime. Initially, I did not want to sleep with the man. He was nice and professional. I made my first payment and agreed to balance up after a few months. As the time drew near and it seems I had nowhere to raise the money, I activated Ada's option. His resistance was minimal as if he was expecting it. The moment we did it, he did not mention fees ever again. I even demanded for receipt for full payment and he willingly gave" Omoni said. "I must say he did a good job. My case was concluded in time. I was impressed and I loved his performance in bed too" she continued.

"Are you paying your lawyer?" she asked

"Yes, I am but he is asking for sex"

"No, you can't pay him and also give him sex. He has to choose one"

"I'm not giving in yet. He is ugly and poor"

"Do you care about his looks? You are simply saving money, there is no sentiment. It's called *fuck-on-the-go*"

"Oh my goodness," I screamed! "Fuck-on-the-go, what a name!"

This must be the trend in this industry obviously. My ears twitched. I was disgusted. Seven women! I was the eighth; our stories were the same with lawyers. I wondered how many more women suffered a similar fate. Our country had better do something about this menace. I could not find any justification for this. I refused to find any. I quickly flipped to the other side. What was the situation with the men folk? Perhaps men paid money while women gave sex. Almost in all things, the unfair treatment of women reared its head. Men are superior. They called the shots.

3

The Brethren and I

FRED WAS AN IT CONSULTANT IN MY FORMER work place. He was signed on a few days after I had tendered my resignation letter. We spoke a few times, I was responsible for explaining the components of the software we engaged him for. I was the business manager. Our brief professional exchanges left great memories.

Three years later, I saw a message from him. I still had his number; he wanted to meet with me. Over the phone in the days before our meet up, he had expressed his desire for a romance with me. I was toying with the idea. He was good looking. We fixed a date for a catch-up. It was a beautiful date. He went about his love for me and how much he had to muster the courage to tell me. It had taken him three long years of contemplation over our brief working experience. He was sure I was his missing rib. I nearly choked with laughter when he uttered this line! What missing rib was this juvenile talking about? I was exactly ten years older than him. I had never been one to date younger men, not even a year younger. I like my men bigger, taller, older, richer and more experienced. Again, this might be wrong. Perhaps, caused by a culture which encouraged the notion that it was a man's world. Fred persisted and pushed me to my wits end. I agreed to meet him again, just to give him a chance to goof. My lady friends thought I should have a go. I did not look my age so if he insisted, I should simply have fun. I was on a journey of self-discovery. I was having another shot at life; this should have been done twenty years ago. Sometimes, I felt like whipping my ass for the time I wasted being the 'good girl'. My friends and I encouraged one another and found safety in our nest. I was set to dump my rigidity to give Fred a chance.

School holidays were still on, he stopped by to see me. It would be his very first time in my home. I gave him a peek into my past and how I ended up alone. "This happened so that you will be for me" he assured. I took his word with a pinch of salt. The City of Abuja is renowned for young men and women who would do or say anything for the sake of getting what they wanted at every given opportunity. He drove a Mercedes Benz. At his age and stage, I felt he was doing well for himself. I never visited his home despite several invitations. As he stepped into my living room, disappointment was written all over his face. The room was bare, at one corner, on the floor, was a nicely made small bed. "Is this your sleep nest?" he asked cynically. "Sure" I answered. "Is this the house you didn't want me to come into?" he continued. If only he knew that this house, the house he looked at with disdain was my palace. If he saw where I was a few months earlier and heard the story of how I made it thus far, he would have been kinder with his comment. I had gone so far, I was no longer one to be beaten down by sarcastic and insensitive remarks. "Come sit down, and make yourself comfortable" I gestured to him as I crouched on my nicely laid out mattress on the floor. He was quick to sit beside me and made sure we had body contact. He placed his hand on my lap. I gently brushed it off. Intermittently, as he talked, he would put his hand over my shoulder or rub my back. For each effort, I rebuffed. He tried every tactic he could but I could not bring myself to lay with a child, and in my mind's eye that's what he was! It wasn't long before he took his leave. I was happy to see him off to this car. He never came back. He never picked my calls afterwards. I was happy to lose him. He must have been a time bomb in waiting, another 'heart break' rocket that would have been launched, so for me, it was a happy shout of good riddance to bad rubbish!

My tentacles have learnt to be wiser and to sense danger from afar. A few things had become clear to me, I was not intrigued by younger men. Again, sex is sacred. I'm not sure I was yet disposed to having indiscriminate sexual relationships. Fred was tall, handsome, well-spoken and attractive enough. He probably was a gigolo who found out that I'm not a goldmine or I spoilt his adventure. I was also on a journey, a journey to find out who I was, and the limits of my freedom, my preferences, taste, style, likes and dislikes. I wanted to know how much a bad marriage affected everything about me. I was happy that I hadn't lost all of my cherished values. I was happy not to be vengeful. I was in complete charge of my faculties. I was happy indeed. I'm not sure about this claim when I'm still in my thoughts. Sometimes, I felt I didn't know what I was doing. I felt I lived in contradiction, confused maybe. I still kept going in the absence of no other option.

While getting over Fred, a church member reached out to me. It was a normal, sunny day that he called.

"Where are you?"

"Wow! To what do I owe this pleasant surprise?"

"But I call you sometimes, don't I?"

"Well, quite rarely but thank you for calling"

"Happy new year by the way"

"Thanks, and you too. I already forgot that the year's still very young and we are yet to see"

"So, what are you up to?"

"Nothing much, I'm trying to figure out what to do. I just got another job, I should resume next week"

"Shall we see then, today, tomorrow?"

"Sure, I hope all is well"

"Yes, all is well. I saw you in my dream"

"Hahaha, it had better be a good dream"

"We were kissing and smooching, hahahaha"

"You can't be serious! Please dream bigger and better dreams"

"Will give you a call, we will see later in the evening. Have a great day"

"Alright, thanks, and see you later"

I was bemused by this call. Prayer, as we fondly called him was not one that kept in touch. We grew a bit closer serving on the church leadership board. He was a devout Christian. I did not know him beyond being a saintly brother in the Lord, a great husband and a dutiful father. I knew a bit of his financial struggles and also when he progressed to build his house. Charles and I considered his family friendly to ours. To my haughty Charles, he was a struggling guy with a civil servant for wife. Charles formed this opinion about him while they sought for a piece of land for their intended home. They (Charles and Prayer) visited many realtors until they settled for one. "If I don't invest this money, I may spend it and I'm not sure when I will have such money again" was Prayer's fear as Charles continued to take him around. Prayer looked up to Charles. In many ways, he found him more exposed, and perhaps richer. Charles knew how to flaunt wealth. He was widely traveled too. It was easy for those who were less well-off to view him as a demi-god. In the course of their quest, their friendship grew but I doubted the depth. I believed they talked men's talk. Our men usually talked about their wives' inadequacies and other challenges they faced at home. I'm not sure what the purpose of this gossip was; women considered them exceptionally gossipy despite their denial. I think men are humans like women. We all talk about people negatively and positively, most times behind their backs. Gossip is not gender based.

Since quitting marriage, Prayer avoided me. I expected more but he gave far less, his attention, calls, moral support: there was nothing I really got to my expectation. He was not the only one, many others had not treated me as I thought they should or would! Again, I take responsibility for this. I was not sure how I was to be treated. I avoided as many people as I could. I retreated into my shell. Church folk in this environment were not that empathetic, so I thought. I was hurting and one of the ways I handled this was to hibernate.

Prayer was sometimes humorous. I brushed off the seriousness of the call and refocused my energy on how the year was going. It was the ninth day of January, and besides getting a new job, I was unsure how the year was going to pan out.

I could not imagine any negative reason for wanting to see me. The dream he talked about must have been a huge joke albeit out of norm for his Prayer facades. I scanned my horizon and concluded this may as well be an answer to my prayer for house rent. My rent was due the following month. I was doing my best to put money together and my efforts were yet to yield a decent result.

By evening, Prayer called for directions to my house. He arrived but refused to park in front of my house. He drove farther away and asked me to meet him in the car. This was my first feeling of uneasy behaviour. I ignored the unsettled feelings in my tummy and went to meet him in the car. He was pleased to see me and asked me to sit in the front passenger seat. It was past 8:00pm and the sky was dark, filled with shinning stars and a half moon. Being in his car suddenly felt strange, I wasn't sure what to expect and why the feeling was such.

"Are you okay?" Prayer interrupted my thought.

"Yes, I am, thanks. Hope your day went well" I reacted

"I see you look well, nicely rounded, chubby cheeks and glowing skin. I'm happy you are doing well"

I was getting a bit agitated. The man I knew never spoke like this. He was usually well composed in words and actions. He was literally very religious. I did not understand this angle. Maybe I was making a mountain of a mole hill. I endeavored to mask my surprise.

"I was thinking of you so I thought I should check on you especially after that dream"

"What dream?"

"I told you I dreamt of you, I meant it. We were kissing and smooching and almost had sex then I woke up"

"You are not serious!"

"I am, in fact, I want the dream to become real that's why I came to check on you" he smiled "Tell me the truth, who has been looking after you? You couldn't have possibly been all by yourself, or are you?" he continued

"I don't understand you."

"What don't you understand, you are a big girl and I want to make it my duty to keep you happy and glowing. Let's not talk too much, kiss me, kiss me baby" he brought his face closer and positioned his mouth.

I was bemused and irritated; I had to calm myself by recalling the hard times I had gone through. Everyone wanted a part of me. I remember Essien telling me that as a single mum, I was old and out of form, I should be grateful to any man who took an interest in me. The reality of life was dawning. Sexual acts were inevitable as far as getting any sort of help from the opposite sex in the city of Abuja. I exhaled and watched Prayer display his wooing skills.

"You want to have sex with me, right? What's in it for me?" I mustered the courage to ask

"I will do my bit, is it not money? I will do as much as I can"

"I need my rent, it is very pressing, very urgent"

"How much is it?"

"Well, I need about two hundred thousand to complete what I have"

"Is that all, that's chicken change"

"I see, bring it tomorrow and you will get your kiss"

"Ok then, see you in the morning, and hope you will be home alone" The conversation eventually fizzled out, I went back home while he drove off. I could not believe what had just transpired.

Suwonki Obatan, aka Prayer, the man next to the Pastor in church, an apostle of holiness, is asking to have me? I could not find words to describe my bewilderment. The next morning, before eight in the morning, he was at my door with the money in a brown envelope. He looked on while I counted. I felt like a whore. This was pure trade and my client was a 'brother in the Lord'. I kept my word. The slut in me woke up, and we had fun doing it and he seemed satisfied and wanted more. And so began our roller coaster adventure. It lasted for almost a year. Sometimes, we left for church from our hotel room. I didn't know how much skill I had acquired over the years. When I saw his wife in church, I suppressed the guilt that reared. I learnt a lot more about men, just being with him. His was a calculated adventure. He budgeted for it and executed his plans with precision. I was impressed!

The downturn was that I reinforced the thoughts that religious people could be fake. The stories that I had heard about pastors getting their members pregnant were not far-fetched. Prayer, was not an ordained pastor. He assisted the pastor in everything; reason why some church members called him pastor. On the other hand, I stuck with him for the crumbs that fell from his pocket. He paid a good part of my bills that year. He was my main gig. I was so focused on him until I had the need to relocate to a better apartment. My eyes were opened to what being a 'big girl' in the city could mean. Some ladies actually lived large on other men. Sadly, this man was a husband to another woman. Life was indeed unfair! One of the reasons I quit my marriage was the inability to cope with Charles' infidelity. Here was I inflicting the same injury on another woman. What reasonable excuse did I have? My heart hadn't become totally stony. I was not proud of myself. I simply needed relief from the never-ending bills! Charles turned his back on us. He made no contribution to the upkeep of the children and me. I shouldered every responsibility and it was getting to me. Now, I could tell the feeling of prostitutes. Perhaps all women at some point in their lives got involved in this trade, implicitly or otherwise. Regardless of all the money that Prayer spent. I never felt love for him. In my heart, I was furious, furious at his deception especially each time I saw him at the pulpit. He said he cared about me hence he came for me. How could I believe the crap? He never spared a dime without having me! I hated what we did but I needed the money. Would this not be lending a hand to the objectification of woman? How could I be indulging in an act that was unbearable to me but for the money it brought. My captor, I dare say, because I was captive to the crumbs that fell from his pocket, he had a field day savouring my body while I languished in guilt and the feeling of debasement. Gradually, I let go of the trade part of the sex, and started willing myself to enjoy it. One day, he opted to use his tongue on me. That was the first day I did not feel like I was doing business with my body. I enjoyed it thoroughly. Subsequent sex became more fun too.

I was happy to be moving some miles away from the home Prayer knew. The former house was within his zone; he breezed in on his way to and from work. I was easy access. We had a hideout, a hotel not too far. It was either we met there or at my home. Gradually, I became what he wanted, his toy, at his beck and call. Moving away from that vicinity was a relief, an answered prayer. In my innermost being, I detested what we did, and sometimes, I told him so. I asked him why he lived such a secretive and amoral life. I sought to know how he reconciled with his conscience and was still able to stand before God's people and preach against the very thing he did. He paid sixty percent of my new rent for me, which was a breath of fresh air. In retrospect, I would never fight a girl who is dating my man, some of them are innocent, intentionally lured. My business should be with my man, my man alone. I learnt also that I could play the game, the game of dating my friend's husband.

Ekpema, Prayer's wife was my sister in the Lord and my friend. We were in the same women's fellowship and served together on a few committees. We visited each other and shared our hearts too. Until Charles and I broke up, Ekpema was one of the women within the church precinct I could count on. She was the epitome of the virtuous woman – submissive to husband, bland taste in fashion, soft-spoken, tongue-speaking, church-going, scripture-reciting and many other things. She was one of those who inspired me to endure hardship and violence in my marriage. To her, a woman, and a Christian woman at that, had to be submissive; obtaining permission for everything she wanted done. I recall some advice she once gave me when I wanted to give away a piece of old jewelry that Charles had got for me.

"Since your husband bought it for you, you need to ask his permission before giving it away," she opined .

"Ask his permission? It's mine."

"But he bought it for you, you should ask him, that's the Christian thing to do."

"I don't get it, am I in prison of some sort"

"But he owns you and everything you have, you should ask him. Anyway, that's what I would do."

I shuddered at her position and stopped asking her opinion on marriage and relationship matters.

Thinking about her husband, I began to doubt the outward

impression she gave us all. She may have been genuine; my business was with her man who had the effrontery to offer me money for my potpourri. Sometimes while church service was on, Prayer would send me messages including X-rated videos. We would keep appointments in our nest, and talk all dirty. I did not know how he managed his emotions. But for me, I felt like an unrepentant sick and dirty sinner.

I recall one of the nights we spent together in a hotel. He lied to Ekpema that he had a business trip, only... I was the business trip. "I've longed to spend the night with you. I've wondered how it would feel having you in my arms all night" he whispered. I hated this! He was a disgusting idiot in my heart. "Look at you, a holy man, and look at what you are doing?" I said to him. In the early hours of the morning, he brought out his bible and, in his manner, as he told me, he had his 'quiet time' with God. I was more confused than ever. A bible in one hand, my breast in the other, I really don't know what Christianity should be! I had what I considered a good Christian foundation. I knew without a doubt that we were both wrong. Sex outside marriage was a sin as far as the faith we professed taught. "How would you manage a man whose wife reports his infidelity?" I asked.

"I would simply tell him what the bible says" he retorted.

"Look, I'm just helping you. You need this. It's taking a lot from me to do this. I'm making a lot of sacrifice. You should appreciate and respect it. This is all for you not me" he continued. I laughed like I had never done before. I would have never imagined such a response.

"Really? For me? You are not enjoying it? You are going against your faith to please me? You are spending your money to make me happy? What's in it for you, hypocrite?" I asked.

"You don't understand; you may never do."

"I pray never to understand. Did you not tell me that your wife does not enjoy oral sex and that you enjoy the dirty things we do? Look at you, I'm sweet if you don't know!"

I believe it must have been a miserable night for him. I taunted him for the hypocritical life he lived. I wondered why he would not come clean so everyone knew what he stood for. We drank alcohol to our fill, and watched pornography. Then, we talked dirty. He shared his escapades with prostitutes with me and how he hoped we could have a threesome. As far as he was paying the bills, my acting skills kept getting better. I considered him an exceptional act too considering that he never gave away his emotions such that his wife smelt a rat. According to him, his wife trusted him the more. He met her needs, he got busier with work and more money rolled in. Whatever was keeping him busy was worth it.

Could it be that money keeps a woman's mouth shut? With money, our men undoubtedly reinforced their supremacy and further subject their women under their feet. If a married woman was making more money, she was unlikely to have sexual relationships with men. With every action, and in every situation, the paradigm 'it's a man's world' was strengthened by both men and women.

I was seriously contemplating stopping church on account of my frolicking with Prayer. My conscience refused to be seared. I was tongue-tied each time I saw him, anger and disdain mixed together brewed in my tummy looking for an escape route through my mouth. The only thing was to stay mute. It bugged me, morning and night.

Just before I quit going to church, a member invited me for the launch of her new business. I attended. It was a successful launch;

the organization was efficient, and effective. It was colourful, and there were local and foreign guests. It looked like a business meeting for the upper echelon of society. I was hoping to get connected, and my desire to stick with the rich and mighty was undaunted. I was basking in this thought when I turned my head. Behold! There were many church folks at the other end of the room. I was immediately put off. I was getting tired of this circle; they smelt hypocrisy or maybe I was the duplicitous one. I made my choice, unfortunately, I did not have much time. It was a morning event; I had taken an hour off work to register my attendance. I could not afford the luxury of staying to the end, especially since they started over an hour behind schedule.

"Our people never keep to time," I remember starting a conversation with the person sitting next to me.

"They are waiting for the ambassadors; they are yet to arrive," she replied.

"Ambassadors?" My mouth and eyes were agape.

"Yes, the French and South-African ambassadors" she said.

"This underscored the quality of people I met here" I thought loudly.

"I don't get you" she replied.

"Not for you please, my apologies, I was talking to myself."

I looked at her and smiled. I needed to estimate her class by her demeanour as if I was psychic. I did not want to leave but I had to. On my way out, I saw a man who had been to my church a couple of times. He waved at me and smiled, I responded before leaving the arena.

At about 7:00pm that day, I got a phone call. "Why did you leave early?"

"Good evening, may I know who I am talking to please."

"It's Pastor Don, we saw briefly at the event this morning."

"Ok but, I don't recall exchanging numbers with you."

"Oh! Sorry I got your number from John, your Pastor's driver". He said he knew you and had your number"

"Ok then, how are you?"

"I'm fine, thank you, you have been out of circulation, I have not seen you, neither have I seen your blue car in a long while."

I laughed at the mention of seeing my blue car. Was I the only one with a blue car? Did he really know me? I did not want to bother my head and progressed in the discussion. I was in a hurry to know what he was up to.

"Yes, I have not been to church for a long time, I'm trying to unclutter my head". The conversation continued for a few minutes. He asked to visit me having taken an interest in my story. I was a dedicated church member. I thought I understood his concern. I thought they were genuine until he visited. He took me everywhere and bought me whatever I asked for. As a test, I asked for nothing, he used his discretion to get groceries; another time, he shopped for clothes. He even got me dildos when I complained of having no male friend. I was unsure what he wanted initially. I saw him as a brother but then, what sort of brother in the Lord got sex toys for a sister? I did not shudder,.We kept playing the game until we eventually made it. This was my very first hit with a man of God. Pastor Don became everything to me, my driver, my friend, my confidant, my brother, my sex partner, name it. He told me about his other flings, he had just broken a ten-year-old relationship for me.

"Well, I don't share, I won't even share with your wife. If you choose me, it had better be only me" I warned him. I was getting stronger in the game, everyone seemed to be on this infidelity path.

I wondered why the idea did not cross my mind while with Charles. I noticed that cheating was the norm in the real world. Everyone seemed to be doing what they liked with whom they liked.

"When did we sell our conscience?" I mused.

Pastor Don became my new automated teller machine. He was timely with his financial services. He gave me as much money as he could access from church offerings. His best days were Tuesdays. He did not give monies on Mondays, he said they were sacred days for him. I believed that was the day he strategized on how much to take from the coffers. The only snag was that he was not as flexible as Prayer. Pastor Don did just one style. He was a terrible kisser. Overall, being with him was lowering my standard as far as sexual prowess was concerned. To think that he was always boastful about how he satisfied his hundreds of women was laughable. This was an ordained pastor; he was happy to date women from all corners. The good thing was that he was handsome, talked in a demure manner and dressed quite well. I did not mind flaunting him as a boyfriend but I could not. He was not only married, but a pastor of an average sized church! As we flourished, I began to have ideas on how to get a bigger fish. "I should get hold of an entire church offering if I get the main man" I thought to myself. I was on a journey of self-discovery. There was no settling for anything less.

"How about your main pastor, I mean the general overseer himself?"

"What about him"

"Does he have side-chicks?"

"I really doubt it. The man seems straight. I have tried all I could to decode his movement, he is straight, he is a real MoG"

"So, you know you are not a real MoG right?"

"Are you God, why do you judge me?"

"Well, I need the main man, I need the real MoG"

"What do you mean?"

"Never mind"

His main pastor, the founder of the church looked sleek, a man of poise and well spoken. I have sat under his voice several times. He definitely had an elite background. I learnt his dad was rich in real estate. He was the heir apparent to the Obidigbo dynasty. Pastor Chuks grew up in the northern part of the country, schooled abroad, had his multi-million private business running simultaneously with the church. He had a great sense of style, when he was causally dressed, he was as simple and expensive as when he adorned in an office suit. I liked him, I admired his composure and sense of reasoning. Hearing that he was conservative, a living example of the faith he professed gladdened my heart. It gave me hope that there were still some good men.

"If it's Pastor Chuks you want to have, just forget it" Don interrupted me. "I have tried him, he is a good man."

"I'm happy to hear that, but are there other pastors like you?"

"Haha, what do you mean like me?"

"Dirty like you of course, worldly, carnal, deceivers …"

"Hehehe, stop it! Are you now a judge, are you God? Is it because I told you?"

"Tell me more, who are the big names in this city who do this?"

"Why do you want to know?"

"I want a part of it, I want to meet them."

"Don't bother, the women are brutal. They surround them and won't even let you near."

"Do you mean their wives?"

Don looked at me cynically. I glanced back pretending to be ignorant of the stories making the rounds. There was nothing new under the sun, not in a city like Abuja.

"What wives? Their wives are certainly not the hurdles. As a matter of fact, their wives are gentle as doves. They hurt no one."

"So then, who, which women are you talking about?"

"Stop acting up my friend, just the way you and me are, would you allow someone else come in between us? Those women will tear you apart!"

"Oh my!"

"Just stay with our level and be content, you may not be able to swim with the sharks. I know you, you are too cool headed to get in the game."

He mentioned a few other well-known pastors and their antics. The stories were gory and discouraging. I wished they were in disparity with the rumours all over the city unfortunately, here was complete confirmation. As a matter of fact, I was in it. For me, I felt like I was in an exclusive caucus. I could no longer speak against them. I had become one of those women too.

"Does your wife know about this?" I queried Pastor Don.

"Erm, she knows because she caught me red handed once, but she doesn't keep it in mind. She knows I have the tendency but I believe she thinks I've stopped it. She caught me a long time ago".

We continued for another year. The money was not as consistent as it was when we started. I got bored too. I wondered what had happened to his generous pocket. I did not know how to ask him. Did I really care about him? Not in the least! If he gave nothing, I would have had nothing to do with him. He was married, he had no direct bearing on my career, what other usefulness was left of him? I knew I was not going to let this stealing slide. I considered it stealing because I knew it was not his money. If he worked in a ? normal organization, he would have been fired and probably jailed. But that depends on who his collaborators were. I believed he must have had a strong ally.

On a certain Friday night, we were relaxing on the couch in a hotel room, his fingers stroking my hair. We had just finished a marathon sexual session, I blurted …

"How come no one ever catches you."

"Sorry" he paused as if he did not get what I said.

"The money, the coffers, the church, no one takes note all these years?"

"I don't understand you."

"You sure do, snap out of the pretense!"

"I honestly don't, please explain."

"How much is your salary? How do you get to spend the money you spend, you drive a luxury car, you keep mistresses, how do you get the money you roll out?" I was point blank.

There was silence for a while, he looked at me as if I had touched the untouchable. By this time, I was sitting and looking straight into his eyes. I didn't want any escape route for him. His long silence meant I had gone overboard, that was my thought. I put my hands on both his cheeks, gave him a soft kiss and whispered in the softest voice "don't worry, we are in this together. I got your back". He smiled and kissed me back with his hands running down my spine, we began to eat another round of the forbidden fruit.

By morning, he made the confession of how he short changed the church. Sometimes, he rewrote the figures after the ushers collected and counted and handed the money over to him. Other times, he disappeared to the toilet with one of the offering bags, empties the proceeds into his pocket and returns the bag. There were times church folk brought him 'pastor offerings' or simply 'blessed' him when he visited them. I knew he was miserly with the truth but then it was not my business. I was simply curious about his financial standing.

This was not my path. I like to flaunt my man. I like to date without guilt, guilt of being with another woman's husband and guilt of spending stolen money. Again, with him, none of my skills were improving, not my communication skills nor my romantic skills. As the year drew to a close, I was set to open another chapter, he was not to be a part of the story. It was convenient while it lasted.

There was a brief stint with Pastor Lafe, a branch pastor of one of the most popular Pentecostal churches in Nigeria. Lafe preferred that I called him without his title. I had met Lafe in the UK about seven years earlier. He was at a conference I attended. He was not a full-time pastor since he was an employee of a university. I held him in high esteem when I saw him at the conference. One day, I needed his help with some office work so I called. He was happy to hear from me. We fixed an appointment and that was how our brief romance kicked off. He was a smooth operator. He knew all the cheap hotels where he took his girls to. I had become one of his girls. For each place, he recounted who he took there and how they operated. I knew I was in deep shit because he would speak of me too! Ours was very brief, his position was very clear, whatever help you need will be exchanged with sex. He didn't give money at all. I considered him very stingy and mean. I dumped his silly ass as soon he was done with his help.

In my quiet moment, I knew that I was reducing my quality of life. I did not think self-discovery meant sleeping with pastors, and every Tom, Dick and Harry. But then, if I did not experience this, I would not know about it. I did not like how I lived regardless of how much it fetched. It simply paid the basic bills and left no room for luxury living. I guessed it was because I was dealing with the less well-known pastors. Surely, the big fish would be richer and more generous, but this was not a life! This was not the way I wished to live. I reminded myself that I was only making ends meet and it wouldn't be for long before I became stable financially. Even then, a lot of adults I encountered seemed to find no wrong in it. Both married and single men and women indulged in extra-marital affairs. It was no news and the silent rule was 'thou shall not be caught'. With the men, they were sure to be forgiven, for a lady it was abominable. She would be exposed and humiliated and most likely sent out of her home.

I was in the web not that the happenings were pleasurable. I probably became a church sleuth. I opened my eyes and ears more to the happenings around. Being naïve was unwise and a disadvantage. It was better to do the things that were appropriate for life's phases and stages.

4

TEACHER IKEDI

I will bring you to your knees Ms Ijendu. I will make you beg and yearn. I will break you, and when I do, I will be satisfied.

MR. IKEDI WAS A TEACHER I ONCE WORKED with, though I was in the administrative department. We had what I considered a good working relationship. He left the school a few months after I joined. I remember his smiles, soft spoken tone, his stout body and funny steps. He was a few years younger than me I suppose. I thought he was a gentleman during the time we worked together.

He had just got married and we were filled with joy at the news of his new baby. He visited me with his wife and their newest addition. Soon after that was the last time I saw him at the school. We soon heard the rumour that he got an offer from a bigger school. We lost contact for many years. Fate brought us back together in another school. I was pleased to work with him. He was consulting for my new boss. We maintained a good working relationship until he started pushing my buttons. In the course of our work, he knew I was off with Charles. I summarised the story for him. I saw traces of Charles behaviour in him. His wife was not allowed to work. Her job was to look after their children since he was away most of the time. I wondered what other jobs he did because it would be rare to have a teacher's salary sustain a family of five like his. By now, any man with bullish tendencies smelt from afar, I despised them, resisted them and I hated to be anywhere they were. Even though Mr Ikedi spoke softly, I was not taken in by his mien. There was more than met the eyes, I knew it was just a matter of time.

Soon, he started making passes at me. He would drop me right in front of my gate after our management meetings. I had no car and my home was along his route. This gesture happened several times. Management meetings held every fortnight for more than a year and for most part, he offered to drop me off. Usually when he dropped me, I thanked him and got out. I was always grateful. I expressed it openly. I never asked him into my house nor offered him a drink, and because I did not bother, he voiced his frustration.

"You don't want to ever ask me in?"

"I'm sorry, guys are not welcome to my house."

"I'm not a guy, I'm your colleague."

"You are a guy, the last time I checked."

"Whatever …"

"Good night sir."

He drove off not wanting to feel defeated. I was obviously mastering the art of handling men. I was never going to be a victim again. My plan was not to be the shaker or stimulator, however, if they provoked me, I would not spare anyone. I did not care that he might not give me a lift me next time. I was put off by his high handedness.

"Why would he not allow his wife to work?" I thought hard.

"He is not that rich!" I voiced this out. "If not for the purpose of putting her down, what could be the reason for not letting her work?" the more I thought about him, the angrier I became. I went inside my house and soon forgot about him. Before long, it was another fortnight. He was generous enough to take me home after our usual management meeting. I did not envisage this kindness after the last experience but then hunters do not chicken out easily. My experiences with men since I got out of marriage had opened my once blinded eyes. My journey of self-discovery had taught me many lessons. Men's insistence to get a woman is not always borne of love. Many times, it's a show of power, they want to be declared the winner. I was not going to give Ikedi the pleasure of winning. If I must, he would bear the brunt of my bad side.

That day, as we drove home, we began to chat, I was bent on probing a little deeper into his thoughts. I needed to know his driving force and his intentions. Did he consider our work, before initiating this game? If the chips were down, who would bear the consequences? Would he deny or not? After a while, my mind went off the corporate imports to pleasure. "Is he big and skilled?

How well could he use his tongue and fingers?" I was beginning to consider using and thrashing him. For all I care, he had no money to dispense so the best he could do, was be an excellent one-off. Again, he was not going to get it on a platter. My house was off limits. If he wanted me, he should know what to do. We were soon at my gate, then he dropped the bomb; "I will bring you to your knees Ms Ijendu. I will make you beg and yearn. I will break you, when I do, I will be satisfied". I knew it! I knew he was a wolf. I smelt it a long time ago. His quiet disposition was a façade. In my heart, I called him all manner of unprintable words. I gently got out of his damned car and banged the door behind me. This was the last of his stupid gestures. At night, that same day, I unbuttoned Ikedi's shirts, I ran my fingers across his chest. There was no hair at all. I told him his chest was not masculine, it was not hairy. I was put off by that already. He apologized and asked me to take him as he was. The chest was broad with two conspicuousnipples. I played with them, he let out a moan. I played the more. He was completely at my mercy, half smiling, half howling. I was in charge. I spent some time on his naval area. There was an unusual depth in the belly-button area. It could hold enough vodka to get me tipsy. I was thinking of pouring wine into it and sipping from it. I kissed it, he let out a sober cry. He certainly was in another world. Then I proceeded to his power house. I was more than bewildered. it was about the same size as my middle finger. I looked at his face, his eyes were closed, his whole body relaxed on my bed. This was the smallest penis I had ever seen. I wasn't sure what to do with it. I was already put off. "How was he going to get me on my knees?" my face dropped and I opened my eyes. What a stupid waste of time imagining nonsense! I heaved a loud hiss; it was the effect of power outage. When I got back home, there was no electricity supply. My upper body was lying in bed; my legs were on the floor. It was meant to be a few minutes rest while waiting for the restoration of power and then my mind drifted. I hated to waste my time on such frivolous imaginings! If the imagination was with a black American president or a parallel celebrity, I would have patted myself on the back. How could common Mr Ikedi occupy my mind this way and for that long? Nonsense! Mtcheeeeeeeeewwww, I heaved a long sigh. It must never happen again, I warned me and assured me all the same.

By this time of my life, I was taking mastery of my emotions. I was learning how to handle the over bloated Nigerian male ego. Charles did enough, Essien completed it, the only option left was to become tough. Our clime is unfriendly to gentleness; it's like a sea of wild fish, a jungle, why should anyone be merciful? I made the choice. In my quiet moments, I realised that this problem was neither about occupation nor riches. Charles was an educated trader, Essien was a lawyer, Prayer dealt in agro business, Don was a full-time pastor and Ikedi was a teacher. Fidelity and sanctity of marriage seem typically far from the husbands in this clime. I should have known, of course I do, I simply forget temporarily. It is a man's world over here. The men know it, they flaunt it. It's in their favour, they uphold it, they shove it down our throats. Of course, we have lived with it, we have accepted it and there is nothing wrong with it. Men make money and spend it on their pleasures which women are a huge part of. The more I thought about this, the angrier I became. I was quick to use abusive words; this is an act I considered awful. I was turning into a street slut. I did not recognise myself. Me? a well behaved and polished girl next door type had become wacky and pugnacious. No! this was not what I had planned for myself. I could not degenerate this badly. I could not disappoint myself and my children. I would not let Charles have the last laugh. The world must never know that our separation took a negative toll on me.

I heard a lot of women did not recover. While with the girls that night, none of their stories was encouraging – Nafisat, Yetunde and Sonia and more girls, they all became wild dogs, an aftermath of a terrible breakup. They tore up homes indiscriminately, flaunting the married men they date. If needed, they confronted the lady of the house, they cared less who was hurting. For them, they had nothing to lose. Oh dear! I always felt this was a huge symptom of a sick life. They are still traumatized, deeply sick and sinking with the emotional ailment, else how does anyone justify the lackadaisical attitude? Where is the dignity? What about sexually transmitted diseases and for how long will a person live off men? I did not want to be like that. I was not wired that way. The more I threw caution to the wind and acted wild, the more I felt dirty; the more I felt odd. I was probably overdoing everything including makeup. I learnt to masturbate. Every night, I was on the internet keeping company with X-rated films. My fingers started discovering my sensitive parts. I got more sex toys and gave myself more pleasure. It felt like I was just becoming an adult. In the day, I was as sane as I could be. I buried myself in work. At night, I was lonely and sad. Thankfully, the children went to a boarding school. They did not get to see the mental state of their mum. But then, some of the other ladies had younger children. I Wondered how they shielded their children from their lasciviousness. I care about the child. A child should not bear the brunt of an adult indiscretion. It's unfortunate that from what I had seen so far, no one really cared about the children, not the society, the stupid society that bore no name. The innocent ones grow up worse than their fathers, they perpetuate the wickedness of society in geometric progression. Their hearts are more hardened than their father's before them. Wait a minute, is this part of the adult life or is it plain heartlessness of our culture? I knew I was sick in my mind. I simply did not know who could help. During my low moments, I fiddled with the concept of wrongness and rightness; what belonged where. I grew up with the bible as the standard. Immorality was wrong in its entirety. I stayed on the path of right living. I kept the rules. There were so many rules in the holy book and in my quest for holiness, I practiced a lot. I had done my best in my younger days.

Looking back, I felt I had wasted my youthfulness. The good girls who kept the laws of the book were not particularly better off and happier than those on the other side of the divide. They did not have the best of husbands neither were they top executives in thriving companies. At best they were managing their lives. I looked around me to see where I had missed it. If God was who we were told He is, why did he not save me? Why did he allow such turbulence to exist in my life? Why did he not magically and miraculously change Charles' heart? Why did He allow me get tangled in his web? While I was troubled inwards, I put up an affectation of calm, especially on Sundays in church and when I met my former church 'colleagues'. I began to view churching as working. In church, you pretend that all is well. You get formal and straight up just like at work. In church, it was all about numerical growth just like the business world. In church new members were celebrated just like a company rejoices over a prospect turned customer. The old members got little attention, they were already consolidated, just like most service providers cared less about already won trophies. Our churches had founders and general overseers, the businesses had chief executive officers, both primarily functioned the same way, they made the final decisions and are key signatories to the company accounts. If you ask me, church is business and business is church.

Edidi was another teacher who further confused my thoughts. Edidi, like Prayer, was a church pastor. Though he was not a full-time employee of his church, he was ordained to occupy the office and bear the title. He knew the bible inside out, appeared gentle and holy, and was inflexible on his religious stance. Edidi spoke gently. He had an overall calm disposition. He prayed fervently and preached fiercely. After each round of sex, Prayer, just like Edidi, will beg me not to let my tongue loose. "If this ever leaks, I will not be able to bear it, please let's keep this a secret", I recalled with nostalgia the few times I threatened to report him to the pastor. He would go on his knees and beg "I'm just helping you, I know you must be missing this so I'm helping you. Please don't let this out, let it be between you and me" he would say. Getting the same bull crap from Edidi was not a surprise. He worked in a big international school. He seemed to have everything going well for him. According to him, he began admiring me the first day he saw me. Unfortunately, I was married and keen on staying faithful. As if he knew what would be, he waited until I broke the news of Charles and I to him. I believe he was happy. At last, he stood a chance! Indeed, he got his chance. He had no thrills and treats. He was too boring to keep a girl on a long journey of self-discovery. Edidi's role in my journey was insignificant. He simply alluded to the fact that church folks are not what they portray outwardly. During the few months we hung out, he added his weight to my teaching career. He taught me a few things, helped me through my master's degree programme, and improved my general leadership skills. He gave me ideas that made me stand out with my boss. I was grateful for his insight. As we progressed, he made some incredible suggestions that threw me off balance.

"Your brain is not enough to keep you going on this job Ijendu, you need something extra," he said.

"Please, don't tell me about God. I know I need Him but just let us be the way we are. I don't want any religious tinge, not right now," I responded.

"Nope, I'm not talking God."

"What then?"

"Do something extra, something deep, something out of your way, do something."

"I'm confused, you haven't said anything yet."

"Being intelligent is good but in today's environment, intelligence is insufficient to get you to the top. You need to be more creative, innovative."

"Something like what please? What do you suggest?" He looked at me as though I was babbling, he shook his head and asked to leave.

"Why are you leaving, are we done?"

"You don't seem interested hence I need to leave."

"How else am I supposed to prove my interest?"

"Think like a mafia, think like a politician, be dirty for once and quit this naïve business!"

"Oh, my goodness! What are you saying?"

"Quit the innocence! Who gets to the top without being dirty? Who stays in a good position in Nigeria with clean hands? Mark my words, you won't survive here if you depend on your intelligence and hard work alone. You won't!"

I tried to be calm and listen. Whatever was making him talk must have eaten deep into him. He sounded bitter, like a person who did not want me to go through what he went through. We both became quiet, our date was no longer romantic, it was rather solemn. The drinks were left standing, the food abandoned. One of my hands was under my chin while the other was on the table, my eyes pierced his eyes through to his heart. I was perplexed. I knew that folk compromise a lot to achieve success sometimes. I'd heard intriguing stories of ladies taking other ladies' husbands, people killing and others visiting sorcerers, magicians, fake prophets and invoking all sorts of spiritual enchantments. I was never one to absorb such fallacies, in my world they were simply myths. Here is a believer in the gospel of Christ, an enthusiastic preacher, a tongue-speaking, demon-chasing, scripture-quoting child of the highest God recommending fetish practices for me to keep a job.

"Surely, there is a lot to learn," I muttered to myself. If this was what it took to be the president of a country or the coolest company in the world, I would have been more interested but to head a school management team? No way! Where would this journey lead me if I followed this path? I was baffled at the same time confused. I didn't get it. "Is this what you did at your place of work?" I finally untied my tongue.

"I'm not in a very high position at my school but I know people who were naïve like you, they all lost out. I also know people who followed this suggestion, they became more powerful. The choice is yours." I heaved a sigh of relief, the fact that the choice was mine was a respite. I kept this idea in my untouchable bag.

5

THE LONE PARENTING VALLEY

IT WAS ABOUT NINETY MINUTES BEFORE MIDNIGHT on a Friday My daughter's temperature rose alarmingly. My heart sank as I thought about my impecunious pocket. The journey of single motherhood is rough in Nigeria. I had weathered the storms for nearly three years. I'm not sure there would be a time to get used to it. Parenting should be for two, this is what my mind tells me. There is no reason for one person to shoulder the responsibility of two. The two decided for a child, the two should bear the obligation. Each morning, I thanked God for good health for the three of us. Sanity of mind and a healthy life were topmost on my daily prayer list. To a large extent, I suppose I had these covered. We were doing fine most of the time. I was grateful.

When Nena was born, we were warned that she was allergic, but the doctor was uncertain of what. He believed that as she grew, we would find out. She was in and out of the hospital. At some point, Dr. Pedro, a stickler for detail, and a jolly good pediatrician, suspected she was asthmatic. She was always on antibiotics. I did not hesitate to administer them immediately I noticed any illness. Luckily, antibiotics were sold over the counter. Self-medication was the norm. It is not recommended but the cost of health care aided the practice. She grew healthily and happily and I had less to worry about. We ruled out asthma and any other respiratory condition. I knew she had tender skin too. Once, we put on an earring, she came out in sores all over her ear lobes. Sometimes, the same sores appeared just at the opening of her nostrils. They were itchy, reddish and blistered. They were most uncomfortable. She also suffered from malaria more than the rest of us. In general, we considered her the most fragile in the house. Her father loved her very much and would not as much as have her feel any pain. Nena was a happy and chubby child. She was a picky eater. We dotted on her and did our best to make her choices available. She and her brother were the reason I stuck with Charles longer than I should have. I feared not being able to cater for their needs.

This particular night, she was sick. We had fared well devoid of hospitals and drugs for more than two years. I don't know why this sickness came on a day I was penniless. I stood outside in tears wondering what options to explore. No mother bears the sight of her sick child. I wiped my tears and put on my thinking cap. I scrolled through my phone and his name popped up again. Essien! I could not help but call the barrister. As soon as I mentioned my daughter being sick and explained how helpless I was at the moment, he swung into action. He went to the pharmacy, one of the good ones that ran a twenty-four hour service. Within thirty minutes, Barrister Essien got to my place. I was very grateful. This was how he found my new place and we rekindled our abusive relationship.

"Look at you, you need me in your life. No other man can have you but me," he boasted.

"Thank you so much, God bless you."

"You didn't want me to know your new place, isn't it? Now I know it. I will visit again and you better tell all those men that visit you to back off, good night," he left for the night.

Him and his thoughts were the least of my problems that night. I was quick to attend to my daughter. A mother will do anything to save her child. By morning Nena was recuperating. Gratefully, we had no need to visit the hospital or spend more money. I learnt that I should not keep permanent enemies. Everyone was important regardless of how unkind they might be. I was not sure about Charles though. For him, I rather he was as far as the sun is from the moon. My feeling was not out of hatred but because I really needed to be completely independent of him. Charles bragged to all and sundry, that I was good for nothing and would be back on my knees because I was definitely incapable of taking care of myself, how much more two children. I was better off begging, cheapening myself with men than enduring the battery from Charles. I'm yet to figure out how I survived the daily humiliation.

As I lay in bed, thankful for my peace of mind and life, I recalled one of his episodes. His brother came visiting. He had spent a few days. Charles and I had a misunderstanding. He threatened that if I left the house without his consent, he would lock me out. I had a friend who was admitted to hospital. It was a Saturday. Charles preferred I stayed home and babysat the children and him. I left for the hospital without batting an eye. By the time I got back, he would not have the door opened for me. I called his brother and he told me how he was not to disobey his brother, "my hands are tied" he spoke in Igbo. I banged on the door until he gave his permission, Steven his brother came to unlock the door. I was furious! As soon as I got in, I demanded an explanation for his act. Before I could end my sentence, I got a very hot slap. I was still in shock when another one landed on the other cheek. I made to retaliate and the beating went on. Charles beat me black and blue, tore my clothes and I was stark naked and crying right in front of his brother. As soon as he was done, he took his car keys and stomped out of the house. I had never been so humiliated.

Embracing single mum status was dreadful. As a child, I had never understood what could justify a woman to be apart from her husband. Besides death, I was sold to the idea that marriage was for better, for worse. I grew up in a society that was unjust to women. It was our fault when our marriage failed and the man's glory when it thrived. From the name a married Igbo woman was called, it was obvious that the society already judged her. She is called 'oriaku' meaning wealth consumer. It is assumed that wealth thrives where there is peace, if she is to enjoy the wealth, she must make all effort to keep peace at home. The entire burden of a successful marriage rested on her shoulders. This is part of the reason leaving is not an option because a woman leaving simply meant she was a failure. The shame that came with it was more than flesh and blood can stand. We were to endure whatever situation we met – cheating, drinking, laziness, beating, abusing, manipulation, impotence, there was no excuse good enough to quit. It was literally for better for worse. Many women did endure, and died in the process. I remember my mum's younger sister, Auntie

Geraldine, we called her Aunty G for short. She was a very pleasant and well-rounded lady. As my mum's younger sister, we automatically loved her and she loved my siblings and me. Aunty Gee never visited our house empty handed. Regardless of how lean her purse was, she ensured she brought bread for her nieces and nephews. She lived in Onitsha, a commercial city in Anambra State of Nigeria. Aunty Gee was married to Uncle Bright; I barely knew him.

My mum and her family could not forgive Uncle Bright many years after Aunty Gee's demise. As an adult, I now understand they had no closure to her death. Her husband did not give a satisfactory explanation on how she died, the police called it a family affair and natural causes, and dismissed the case. She was buried amidst many unanswered questions.

Aunty Gee, a beautiful and bubbly woman visited her mum, my grandma from Onitsha. Her protruding tummy showed she must have been over six months gone. Everyone was ecstatic at the expectation of a new addition to the family. Since Onitsha was not far from the home of my maternal Grandma, she visited to show herself. This was the best form of breaking the news of pregnancy. They spent Saturday night together. Granny pampered her; they caught up on so many stories. Everyone was happy. If only they knew that these were their last moments together! No one had an inkling that Uncle Bright and Aunty Gee did not live happily. Women were not allowed to show the bad sides of their husbands anyway, I believed she came out to get a breath of fresh air before returning to her captor. Unfortunately, granny did not pick up on this.

On Sunday morning, the news of her death reached us. Uncle Bright said she died in her sleep but we did not believe him. Uncle

Kanna, mum's older brother lived in Onitsha too. He was working with a thriving pharmaceutical company so we considered him rich. He was well educated too. According to his narration, he went over to the house where Aunty Gee lived with her husband and a young son. One of the neighbours, a woman who preferred to be anonymous told of how they heard Aunty Gee wailing and asking for help in the middle of the night. "He beats her almost every night. We hear her cry, we always do!" said Uncle Kanna as he quoted the anonymous neighbour. "We believe Geraldine died during or after the beating. She was pregnant and he was beating her. That man is the killer." We were all broken at this news. Uncle Bright looked very innocent; just like Charles. His demeanour appeared staid. I would have regarded him as the gentlest man on earth. Thinking about him as I write this, I remember how I viewed Charles. Uncle Bright spoke very few words and dished smiles generously. From a distant, we all thought Aunty Gee deserved such a cute and loving man!

As culture demanded, he was to come home and formally tell the family what had happened to the daughter whose hand he had asked for in marriage. This is the part of our culture I love.

A man takes his family and humbly visits the home of his intended wife, he bows and requests for permission for her hand in marriage. He does not come alone, he comes with respectable and older members of his family. The woman is handed over to the eldest relative of the man who accompanies him for the marriage rites. The woman's family elders request the elders from the man's family to take care of their daughter. This is symbolic, the husband is the one to sleep with the woman but no, he alone is not responsible for her. The whole family is. They will be accountable in the event of anomalies. This makes me emotional. It depicts that marriage is sacred, it binds families, it is not a one-man business. There are stakeholders and shareholders hence dividends ought to be shared by all those involved. Marriage is good and honourable, I feel that some unscrupulous elements who derive joy in deriding women undermined it for their own gain. They stripped people of the joy, productivity and tranquility that come with equity and fairness rather than objectification.

Uncle Bright came, he came with two of his kinsmen on Monday evening. Before his arrival, Uncle Kanna had briefed the family of his findings. Aunty Gee was healthy, she spent Saturday night with Mama, she left for Onitsha which was approximately thirty minutes away on Sunday afternoon. By Monday morning, she was dead according to her husband. Uncle Kanna came home to be with his mum, my granny. He knew the Udeze family where Aunty Gee was married into would make an appearance. They had an explanation to give and we were anxious to hear their side of the story. She died a pregnant woman though young. There was no need to delay her interment.

Before the sun went to bed, they arrived, three solemn looking men came through the entrance gate.

Grandma's house was a few metres inside the compound. From a strategic corner of the house she could see anyone who entered. This was a norm in those days. The patriarch usually acted like the chief spiritual security officer, making sure that whoever accesses the gate is duly captured. She saw them and before they reached the mud house, she was in the living area waiting for them in tears.

"*Nne ndewo[1],*" greeted Uncle Bright.

---

[1] ***Nne ndewo** – Greetings mother*

"*Ogo, imela*[2]," followed one of the kinsmen from the Udeze family.

"*Mama, ndo nu*[3]," completed the third man.

"*Nno nu, oche di*[4]," said Delunebe, my strong hearted grandma.

Everyone sat quietly, one could hear the sound of a pin drop! Ikem, being the oldest spoke on behalf of the visitors.

"*Ogo m*[5], we are deeply sorry for what happened. Words cannot express it enough. We came for her because we believed she will complete our son and bring joy to our family. We believed we would care for her and live with her till old age. We hoped she would bear us children and nurture them till adulthood. Fate has tricked us. Death has cheated us. Our hearts are very heavy; we are not able to find the right words to break this news to you. Our wife, your daughter has gone back to her maker. She left this morning.

There was a heavy sigh from Uncle Bright, his head bowed and tears flowed freely. I believe he must have been in shock. He didn't anticipate the turn of events. I doubt that anyone marries a partner with an intention to kill and even if there was an intention, not from beating and not with an almost completed pregnancy. I felt for him. Delunebe's head was bowed. She had tears coming down her cheeks too. The fingers of both hands were clipped and laid on her wrapper-covered thighs. After a moment of silence, she raised her head and looked directly at Uncle Bright.

---

[2] ***Ogo imela*** *– My in-law greetings*
[3] ***Mama ndo nu*** *– Mama, peace to you and yours*
[4] ***Nno nu, oche di*** *– You are welcome, please take your seat*
[5] ***Ogo m*** *– My in-law*

"*Nwa m, biko*[6], tell me exactly what happened. She was here with me on Saturday. She was healthy and cheerful. She was happy. What really happened?"

"Mama, I cannot tell. I woke up this morning, she was still asleep. I waited for her in the living room until 6:30am when she usually wakes up but she did not. I went to wake her up and she would not respond. I raised an alarm with my neighbours before rushing her to the hospital," Uncle Bright answered.

"You mean she died in her sleep? How did you people sleep the night before? Was there any quarrel, any fight, any argument?" Grandma continued.

"Hmmm, we slept like a man and wife sleep. I did not really play the game with her. Since she took in, she complained more of discomfort so I usually leave her alone whenever I want to touch her and she declines. Last night, we laughed and joked and disagreed a little just like husband and wife do before we slept."

"What did the doctors say?"

"By the time we got there, she was already gone for a few hours. They confirmed her dead and we headed to the mortuary."

"But …"

"Mama" Edozie cut in, "Shall we question God who gives and takes? This is a very hard pill for all of us. The more we ask, the more we will get pained, the more we habour anger and bitterness. As a person, I'm yet to believe it. I called her Gerry, she was my wife. She was a good woman; this is evident in the manner she chose to leave the earth. She left peacefully in her sleep". He raised his head up and said "God you know why this befell us. We shall not question you. We know you can see our hearts and our pain. Please comfort us"

---

[6] **Nwa m, biko** – *My son, please*

"*Ndi ogo m[7]*", said grandma "you must pardon me but I think we should report this matter to the police. There should be an investigation then we can talk about the burial."

This last request from Delunebe threw the meeting into pandemonium. The three men did not expect it. They were displeased and did their best to dissuade mama who would not bulge. Eventually, aunty Gee was buried, relationships went sour.

My mother never forgot this. For her, it was better to be alive and out of marriage than to be married and dead. She was against physical abuse. I endured physical abuse from Charles, I did not let mum know. The day I garnered courage to tell her was the day she reminded me of aunty Geraldine and told me without mincing words to leave without looking back. My father was long gone from earth so her decision was usually the final. My brother Ugo was in support. I was glad to be alive and sane. I simply did not imagine the roughness of single parenting. I could brave all other struggles, but watching my child sick and being helpless was the height!

Some months later, I got back from work to see Ide lying helplessly on the bed. My heart skipped.

"What's wrong?"

"I don't know, my tummy hurts," I barely heard his faint voice.

"Oh, my goodness, when did this start? What did you eat?" I made to help him sit up and plan the next course of action.

I looked at his tummy, it was bloated and swollen. Thankfully, I had some money. I dressed him and we headed for the hospital. The first doctor examined him and said she suspected inflammation of one of the organs. I died on hearing this. The only

---

[7] *Ndi ogo m* – *My in-laws*

thing I consistently asked of God was sanity of mind and good health. I always knew that I could not deal with sickness. I had never known how to deal with it. I was not about to begin learning it.

"God you know my strength; you know this is not it. I can't deal with this; I can never deal with this" I was shouting. She referred us for further tests and prescribed drugs to ameliorate his pains. It was a big government hospital. We proceeded for the tests. I had to make immediate payment for the tests else hospital protocol would have prolonged my son's pain. I had to be strong for him. I had to be calm for him. I had to be his succour and give him the hope of being alive and well. This was one of my lowest points since being a single mother. It was an emotional upheaval for me. We pulled through. He had nothing serious, all the organs were functioning well. He had eaten too much beans and suffered from bloating or whatever the doctor explained. My joy was that there was nothing complex and we could go home that night.

My experience so far was a show of uncommon determination. It was filled with constant competition within myself to stay afloat "He won't meet me where he left me" was my mantra. But then, who was I competing with? What sort of stress was I subjecting myself to? Did the marriage end and I'm still in it? Is this how to discover myself? When people get abused, they may flee from the abuser, but most often they need detoxification. I noticed I was constantly fighting with myself. I never bothered to give me a treat. I was always on edge and never looking at things positively. I guess I was completely battered and traumatized. I recalled the night I had to attend the inaugural party of his excellency. I was to pick up my friend, Nnedi. I got to her house, called her to meet me at the car park. I waited.

After waiting for nearly thirty minutes in the car. I made a move to find out the exact situation of things. I was super angry considering that I was a stickler for time. It had taken practically all my life to master the art of being on time. Everywhere I went, I was renowned for it. This attribute stood me out, and got me several awards. I was happy for it and for each new appointment, I aimed at outdoing myself. I may not be the first at work but definitely, I was never near late. I took no excuse for lateness either. I recall I was nicknamed 'clock' by my secondary school peers, a name that trailed me as I advanced in life. "Where is it?" I heard a yelling voice "I said who took it? Where did you keep it?" her voice was thunderous. I stood still by the door for a while. "What could they be looking for? How could I interrupt? What was I to do?" I was mussing, then came a loud bang on the table "if I don't see this ring today, you and your brother will be in hot soup. Who told you to go to my dressing table? Who asked you to touch my things? Look for it, search everywhere, find it. You know I cannot leave this house without it …"

I knocked on the door and pushed it open. I walked in gently wondering what ring could be causing such a dichotomy between mother and sons. As soon as Nnedi saw me, she became agitated.

"I'm so sorry babes, forgive me."

"What's wrong? What is happening?"

"It's my ring, I don't know where these boys threw my ring."

"What ring?"

"You know I have to wear my ring for an occasion like this, ah! (she crossed her two hands over her head), there will be dignitaries, won't there? How will I attend such a function naked?"

"Honestly, Nne, I'm lost, what exactly are you talking about? You are not naked; your dress is beautiful and classy and expensive looking…"

"You don't understand"

"What don't I understand?"

"Syl, Chess, have you found it? Check under the bed, the table, the chair, lift the books by the bedside table one by one, and very carefully too," Nnedi screamed at her sons.

"What the heck are you doing? Don't you care if we are late? I should not have come to pick you up."

"Pls don't be angry, it's my ring, I feel naked without it. I need to use it."

"What ring?"

"My band of course."

"What band are you talking about?"

"The one I always wear, you are my friend, please understand."

"I really wish I do. Can you please calm down and let me know what exactly you mean?"

"Hmmmm" she heaves a sigh "It's my wedding ring. I can't dress like this outside and look like a single lady, I can't."

"Oh, my goodness!" I stomped out of the house. I angrily got into my car as I slammed into reverse gear, there was Nnedi at my rear. She walked to the side then to my window.

"Please don't be angry. I expect you to understand. Please my dear friend, understand."

"I do, I really understand. That is why I will be going to the party without you. You can find your way when you find your ring. Come in your birthday suit wearing just the ring. See ya!"

I zoomed off. I could not understand Nnedi. She had been apart from her husband for about eight years. The man is happily married to another in Lagos while she stays in Abuja deceiving all and sundry that she was still married. I was furious that she had almost made me late for the inaugural ball of his Excellency.

"Stupid girl!" I screamed as I drove off.

Nnedi was not alone in this sort of behavior. Oganya had a similar mindset. Under 'marital status' of all forms she fills, she ticks 'married'. She does not believe she is divorced because her kinsmen have not returned her dowry according to custom. His people warned her to comport herself properly as Uzo's wife. They would not like to associate her with wanton living. She was reminded that she is a mother and by all rites and customs a married woman. Her utterances, outlook and actions must rhyme. She acquiesced. I tried to dissuade her. I really tried.

"Live a real life and not a mirage," I constantly chided her but the voices of her people were stronger than mine. But then, did I not consider those that made a choice of living like single ladies a wild one? Perhaps it was because they toyed with husbands and not single men. Sometimes, I feel I'm confused in my thoughts!

I embraced my status as a single mum wholeheartedly. I regarded myself as a divorcee, the lady with an unsuccessful marriage before a friend put the phrase 'single mum' on my lips. I was proud to be one. I simply had the problem of adjusting to providing for two on my own, and most especially giving them the quality of life, they were used to.

Sometimes, I barked at the children when they ate huge portions of food. I got upset if there was no money and they made a simple demand of going to the cinema or having an ice cream.

"Did you ask if I had money?" I would scold "Next time, ask if there is money before you make any request. I told you guys to be prayerful but you never pray, and then you expect good things. Where on earth do you expect me to get money from to sort you out?" I made them edgy in their own cocoon. Where else would they run to? I wanted to have custody. I kept them to prove a point and here I was making them miss their father and wishing for our former home.

In the third year of this journey, the long holiday was almost over. I was apprehensive again. I didn't understand my constant worry whenever there was need to spend money, especially a bulk sum. I had spent so much ensuring that the children had great fun, we visited places, had holiday lessons, bought clothes, shoes and all sorts. They were happy and so was I. I was working my way to their hearts, to renew their trust and keep faith in me. I believed I succeeded that holiday, but when it was time for school, I did not have their fees. My thoughts could not come up with any reasonable strategy to make more money. It was difficult living within my income. Does anyone actually live within their income in Nigeria? This is the reason for the indelible corruption the country is known for. I got a piece of paper and took out my phone. I began to write down names of all the men who had ever 'toasted' me. My plan was to ask each person a certain sum hoping that in total they will make up the sum I needed. What a fool's paradise! All failed! Not one person on the list offered as small as a thousand naira. It was as if they knew I was up to something. Foolish me, the same energy had used to think up such stupidity could have been put to better use! I was frustrated, extremely so. I traded their fees for fun and I thought I could have my cake and eat it. Sometimes, I feel that a single mum may need the perspective of a male after all. The Maker, as we were told made man male and female.

I compared being with Charles, and being alone, I could understand the reason more abused women would rather stay in a marriage than break up. There is a shield it probably gives. It makes a woman fully relaxed in her comfort zone. I was torn apart! From married men who considered they were doing me a favour by dating a mother of two, to single younger men who thought they would be my handbags feeding off my hard-earned money. As soon as they found out I was alone in my house, they wanted to pitch their tents. I always insisted that men do not sleep in my house. I do not harbour them; I do not even as much as have sex with them in my house except they are paying the bills. I could tell the implications; they would live off me and become a clog in my wheel.

As I contemplated the lows of my journey, I cried but I was at peace. I never regretted ending my relationship with Charles. It was good it ended. I would rather have the turbulence around, most of which was financial, but peace within, than otherwise. There were many moments I felt incomplete being without a man, my pillow soaked up all my unsaid thoughts and my river of tears. My pillow, my closest ally understood my low moments more than anyone. My pillow never judged me, it never talked back and never condemned me. It was always soft and tender and always there for me. My pillow never shoved me or pushed me. It never got tired and never gave up on me. My pillow knew the many times I cursed Charles and all other men. It did not keep a record of the number of times I sighed looking at the bills and wondering how to sort them out. It did not reveal how often I planned robbery in my mind, robbing a bank, a sole business or an individual. My dearest pillow, my confidant knows how much I loved my children and how, at the same time, I wished they could be adopted by a rich and kind man just for me to have breathing space. This pillow and I had a pact; no one could know when I hadn't brushed my teeth because the last bit of money in the house had been used to buy palm oil instead of toothpaste! My pillow bore the smell from my mouth as I soliloquised. It could not tell anyone that the bedsheet complained of my farts from the constipation of eating only beans because I had no money for a good meal. What about my hair? There were many times I wore the same hairstyle. I could not afford to visit a salon for proper treatment. It came out, It smelled. It dripped of oil from a constant application of hair cream, which was one way I preserved its look. My pillow is my closest buddy, it never washed my dirty linen in public.

Being a single parent is a hard task, a really hard one. I made all the decisions, from the haircut style to where to visit for the holidays. Sometimes, I had to rent a daddy figure to give pep talks. I was the handy man, a carpenter, an electrician, a plumber, and a tailor. I was dad and I was mum all day, all week. The children's needs were first followed by the common needs then mine, but where are the resources to meet my needs? There was the lingering battle to stay well behaved to avoid being talked down on. I learnt from my friend in Lagos that some landlords would not rent out their properties to a single mum even if affordability was not a problem. A lot of them resorted to hiring husbands.

"This must be a booming business by now; husbands for hire, pay hourly or daily," I made a joke with her as she recounted her experience. She had to get a friend to pose as a husband in order to sign the rental lease. She had such a great laugh having made a fool of the landlord.

6

A Young Doctor's Gentle Touch

I MET EMMANUEL ON ONE OF THE SOCIAL MEDIA platforms. Apparently, he saw my argument on a thread and considered me intelligent enough for a closer chat. He insisted on being my friend. I was hesitant because I felt he was a bit young, and I was unwilling to offer what he would want. I knew he was going to ask for more than a platonic relationship from the way he pushed. As a matter of principle, I don't date a man one day younger than I am. This was the reason I broke up with Igoni, the moment I found out his age, I retracted. I refused to give him my reason, he got tired and left me. Igoni was a year younger. Here comes Emmanuel, a medical doctor from the eastern part of the country, another whooping ten years younger than me, it was a complete out of bounds situation except I wanted a toy to play with. I had tried this with Fred, it backfired. Emmanuel would not give up. To him, he was more than equal to the task. Dr. Em as I called him was cool, calm and collected. He was a good listener, hardly argued. When listening, his gaze was strong, he leant forward with rapt attention. Most times, his face was blank giving no clue to his thoughts. He was a gentleman by all standards. I remember our very fist date.

It was an exclusive and expensive restaurant in a high brow area of the city. I was there before he arrived. We sat at a table for two and placed our orders; my drink had a bit of alcohol while his didn't. He said he was off alcohol at the time. He'd had a little too much while in medical school. He was the life and soul of the party back then. As he talked, I was imagining what his life was. Indeed, experiences have different effects on all of us.

I probed further about his life; he did not have more than three- or five year's post-graduation experience. He lived in the suburbs, had no car, he was practically starting life. I decided to be his friend, there was not going to be an amorous entanglement. I kept to it. We were very good friends. We had sufficient time to chat, especially when he was on night call. This singular meet-up on this fateful Sunday evening made me review my thoughts on the male gender. We talked about his past, present and intentions. He was very generous with information about his life. As soon as it was my turn, I could not reciprocate. I was unsure where I was headed. I took pride that I worked in an international primary school and that was to suffice. The school offered me what he called peanuts considering the number of years since I'd left university. He asked about my future plans and I went blank. He must have been disappointed. I told him where I was coming from and he asked how many years I had been a single mum. To my surprise, this young man was interested in my wellbeing not my money. He did not talk like a typical young Igbo man.

Igbo men are averagely pompous and rarely have regard for their woman. Most often, they parade themselves as superior, next to God. They act accordingly too. I recall when Barister Gbenga, the gritty lawyer who withstood Charles' calumnies and coercions against me, reported Charles to the police department for bigamy. He was arrested, and indeed he bragged about his act. "I am a titled Igbo man, I'm entitled to as many wives as I want". The investigating police officer was taken aback; his surprise was how a man who married under statutory law did not realise that bigamy was a criminal act and yet he took pride in breaking the law. This was nothing compared to how some of the men negatively interpreted a rich culture that paid handsome respect to women, for their personal aggrandizement. Dr Emmanuel won my admiration instantly! Being a man and a doctor was enough reason to be a self-assured hubris. But he wasn't in the slightest like that. My brain quickly ran through the flavours of the vampires in men's bodies that had passed through my life in the last few years, Dr. Emmanuel stood out. We talked, drank and kissed. This was the highlight of the evening! He deserved that kiss. It was a kiss of appreciation straight from my heart. He was worth dating and keeping. It was a gentle, lasting, hot-blooded, luscious, voluptuous and sizzling kiss. I didn't want it to end as our lips locked for a few minutes. He held me tight, I reciprocated. In between the kiss, we stole a glance at each other with one eye. Deep kisses are sweeter with eyes closed hence we had to steal glances. He kissed the tip of my nose, my forehead, my cheeks and my lips. When we unlocked, he held my palm, clasped it gently and kissed its back. I was over the moon! Just before he got into the taxi, he hugged me one more time and a short kissing game ensued. My heart melted for him and I wished he was my knight in shining armour. The evening ended well beyond my expectations. We bade each other goodbye as he hopped in the back of the taxi.

I had to rethink my life. It was the 28th of December; I was happy that I'd given him an opportunity to offer healing words and guidance. I knew I had to come down from my lofty height and face the real person. My only problem was that he did not have the financial security to support me. I needed money. I came clean with him. "I don't want to date you, you don't have the means to support yourself and then me" I said to him. He was taken aback by my statement. "Support you? Are you looking for financial support? Is that what a relationship means to you? Money?" he sighed. "I'm a bit disappointed girl" he continued. "Please stop it" I hushed him. "What else do you have to offer me" I asked.

"And what do you have to offer me?" he retorted.

"What? You expect something from me? Something like what?

"Oh! Was I going to give and you will not give something in return?"

I became instantly dumb! Someone had pressed a reality-check-button. What do I have to offer to myself and to others? What does my fragrance say? When I step in and step out, what impact do I leave behind? My head spun three hundred and sixty degrees just like an owl.

"I'm sorry. I need to sleep, good night."

Our phone conversation ended abruptly. We started the chat on his way home and before he got home, I was getting reset. I turned off my phone and tried to get some sleep. Sleep eluded me. I started counting numbers until I lost consciousness. The next morning, I turned on my phone and saw his message; "baby, you are much more than you think about yourself. You have a lot inside of you, why lock them up? Unleash them, unleash every one of them. Fly, the sky is big enough, it can take you and others. I may not have money to give you but I have ideas. I have protection. I have your interest at heart. I have the male perspective to things. I'm sorry, I don't want to date you. I can't date an insecure woman. See you at the top!" This was the final blow. Someone had given me the description I needed. I was an insecure woman. I was emotionally unfit for any serious relationship. All those men probably treated me that way because that was the air I gave off. I knew I had to find help because I could not help myself. Where was I going to find the help I needed? How much would it cost? I did not want to ruin my life. I felt bad losing a young man who could have added colour to my insipid life. I called him back but he would not take my calls. He was done for real. I cried, I cried so bitterly on my pillow. My ever- faithful pillow.

"Please take my call, please, give me one more chance. Help me rebuild. Please I need you," I sent these lines to him.

"I'm sorry, I'm a doctor not a therapist. I'm unable to help you. I am young and have my life ahead of me, I can't jeopardise it because of you. Look for help, search social media, I'm sure there will be free help here and there for you. Make use of it. This is the last I will communicate with you. I will block every avenue of communication with you henceforth. Trust me when I say you need emotional help, you do. You won't make much progress without it. I love you. Doc."

This was the shortest diagnosis I'd ever had, an honest truth from a man I looked down on. In his rejection, he was calm and kind. I was at my lowest ebb. I remembered what Dr Ene had told me the moment she heard Charles and I had parted. "Ezinne, do not have another serious relationship without therapy. I had to have some and it indeed helped me". Dr Ene was a lady I met in a church. She was a lecturer in the school of medicine at the university. She got a scholarship and travelled overseas for further studies. While there, she had her husband and children join her. We wished them well and hoped for the best for her family. A little less than two years of her family joining her, we got the news of their separation. Obed her husband was back in Nigeria with unpleasant tales of their union. I was devastated. Ene was a spiritual sister. She was an example of a virtuous woman. She won my admiration from the way she spoke, she dissected the bible and prayed fervently. I could not fix the puzzle no matter how much Obed explained. This marriage should not be over. We kept hope alive and wished for the best. Four years after her incidence, mine happened. I did not know how she heard because she was not in touch with me. She severed most relationships. I had no clue of where to get any information about her. She went off social media. She changed her phone numbers, and never replied my emails. I quit trying to get in touch. One evening while I was relaxing, her call came through. She hid her number, so I could not tell what country she was calling from.

"Ezinne (this was the pet name she called me while we served in children's church), how are you? I heard what happened. How are you and the children?"

"Eneayi, is this you? Oh, my goodness, it's nice of you to call. I'm good. How are you."

"I'm good, the children are too."

"Who told you about me? Where have you been?"

"That's not important. I just needed to touch base with you. You are my friend and I've been through this. Look, get therapy. Don't get into another relationship without having therapy. It will do you some good else you will have similar problems in another relationship." "Therapy? What do you mean?"

"It's that simple Ezinne, you need to talk with a professional counselor, not a psychiatrist."

"They are expensive, I can't afford one."

"Try, save for it. Pay in bits, it will do you good. Just don't get into another relationship without seeing one. I have to go now. I will call again."

"Wait, please don't go ..."

"I will call again, bye."

The line went off. This was one of the earliest pieces of advice I got. Most others told me to rebuild my life and focus on getting empowered. To many people, if I had the financial muscle, Charles would not have treated me the way he did. Things would have been a little different. Dr. Ene was a medical doctor, she was financially independent, and she had little good to say about her estranged husband. If she narrowed on mental wellness then I had to heed. Events overtook this suggestion as I hustled for survival. I did not have any extra to give a therapist. I had to first of all think of daily meals for the children and me. Charles had abandoned us to our fate. I bore all expenses. Reading Dr. Emmanuel's last message, I knew that I must seek help. It was inevitable.

The rest of the year ended quietly. I was deep in thought for the remaining days and in the early days of the next year. I needed to get a therapist. I needed to chart a course for my life. I needed to be well, fully well as the bible said - spirit, soul and body. I had stopped going to church as I felt I was not getting anything from it. Again, Prayer was a member of this church. Seeing him upset me thoroughly. I could not bring myself to tell the pastor what happened neither could I bear seeing him on the pulpit sharing the word of God. I knew life was not black and white but then, I could not adjust to the deception all around me. I am a straight forward brutally honest fellow. I played pranks but not for long else I would be caught. I stayed in my lane and doffed my hat to those who competed in the dogged and illusory race. I accepted this was not my call. 'Who will help me' became top on my priority quest. I began my search. I told anyone I could, that I was in search of a shrink. Some laughed and others empathised with me. While in search, a friend added me to an all ladies virtual group. I was amazed at the level of openness I noticed. I was definitely not alone. I stayed, I sucked up as much as I could from their stories and deliberations. I made some friends too. This became my very first therapy – hearing from fellow women in a nonjudgmental fashion was uncommon. Those who dared judge were banned and those who could not speak like me were encouraged. The aim was to banish the culture of silence that was prevalent in our clime. The group grew, and so did my knowledge. I learnt empathy and being free-spirited from the group. The more I took in, the more I changed. The more I could keep relationships. The more I held people accountable. The more objective driven I became, and lived purposefully. My entitlement culture began to dwindle. My pillow had fewer tears to worry about. My children began to experience a happier mum. I was changing in and out, even with my dressing. I was becoming self-aware. I read stories of women in worse situations than mine. I read how they picked themselves up and how they were in their dedicated lanes pursuing their courses. I read about the progress they were making. I was encouraged. The more I took in, the better I felt, the bolder I became, the happier, andmore vibrant and productive I got.

Being in high spirits is attractive, and opens up the brain for ideas. It repels depression, brightens the mind to opportunities. I started getting business ideas; I registered a company. I was not just thinking about things, I was implementing them! Hustling became less stressful, money became my friend. I saw the difference between being moody, confused, cantankerous and being self-aware. The later made one happy from within, while the former left you perpetually putting up a façade, staying defensive and dispersing negative energy. I had taken a step in the right direction for the first time since my separation. I started thinking of a makeover; I needed to change my look, my hair style, my dress style, the way I spoke, and my gait. I knew this was another uphill task as it would require a lot of resources. I simply kept hope alive. The good book which I was raised with tells me that hope does not disappoint. I held unto this tenaciously.

Dr Emmanuel's thought stayed with me. I was beginning to fall in love with him long after he was done with me. He was different from all indications. I looked at his picture every night, I noticed his beautiful features, his smile was broad and his eyes sparkled. He dressed well and his shoes looked expensive. I remembered his gentility and how he stroked my hair the night we kissed. He was a clean and confident man. I imagined how he would have given me satisfaction had we gone the whole way! I felt bad that I lost this man who had been genuinely interested in my happiness and security. He was the only man I had met who didn't go straight to sex talk or remind me of how I was a single mum needing help. He believed in me, didn't want me to be filled with excuses to remain impoverished. I think he was an angel. His thoughts were memorable, I cherished them, I bore them in my deepest being. I hope that someday in this life, I would see him, he needs to see how much I have healed and succeeded.

The need for a therapist became paramount as well. One thing was certain, I was not going to have any real relationship until I met with a therapist. In my subconscious, this remained, while I carried on my daily activities. Besides heeding advice from the two doctors, I did not want to ever lose a great friendship as a result of my mental state.

Unfortunately, therapists were rare in this part of the world. Most people referred me to some untrained bible preaching elderly men and women in church who themselves needed therapists. The concept of seeing a therapist was alien of sort. I recall how an enlightened colonel in the Nigerian army went hysterical when I mentioned a need for therapy. He lost his wife of four years to death. "I've grieved for a year and moved on; if I can move on, who can't? There is no big deal about your marriage crashing, you'd better save the money and use it for something worthwhile" this was his position and he felt he made a sensible point. He, like many others, do not consider trauma as a situation that needed to be managed. It became worrisome to me that as enlightened as we were in our country, this subject was untapped.

7

MY RUTHERLESS LIFE

AS A GROWING CHILD, I HAD DREAMT OF becoming a medical doctor. I considered myself resilient enough to handle the hard work that it required. I sat and passed the national common entrance examination that got me admission into a prestigious federal government college. Many people did not pass such examinations at that time. It was highly celebrated in my house and set me apart from my siblings. My parents did their best against all odds to ensure I attended. Despite the school being in another state to the north, my dad was not dissuaded. He wanted the best for his daughter. According to him, "if her brain got it, then we have to support her", this was his answer to my mum when she expressed her anxiety over my going to a boarding school in a faraway state with no relations. They took me to school, got me settled in and left with a promise to visit before the term ran out. My dad, the best dad anyone could have, kept his promise. He visited. He made sure I was doing well.

The journey into my life's destiny was about ten years old, nine of the years were spent directly under my parent's breast. I was beginning another phase, this was a joint tutelage. I was learning independence, making fundamental decisions and managing my finances during the term while I reverted to their authority during the holidays. I liked the challenge. I did not do as well as I was expected; then I picked up. I chose the sciences for my senior secondary school subjects. I was heading to be a doctor so that was the only choice. I tried my best, I worked as hard as I could but I did not make the general certificate examinations. My result was not good enough to admit me into the university. I became depressed. Worse still, my parents were mad, their only hope was dashed. I did retake the exams, I failed again. The result I got could not get me into my choice course, I failed physics and chemistry which were core subjects for any science course. I did not press further, I settled for the next available course, a business management course. My beloved father had taken ill. The sickness was taking its toll on his productivity. Money was becoming scarce. My mum was a sit at home mum looking after eight children. My sweet dad bore the load of bearing all the bills. Right now, with just two children, I imagine what he went through. I feel sad that he died before we could give him a deserved accolade. Long after his death, we were living off his hard work. We did not pay rent. We had to sell a few of the properties he left behind in order to survive. God bless my dad!

So, I finished the course at university and had no clear-cut direction of what I wanted to be in life. Perhaps, I was in a hurry to get through school hence I settled for less than I should have. Looking back, I feel wasted, sad, unfulfilled. I feel lost. I felt depressed. The chief cause being that I was unsatisfied with my life's trajectory. Starting afresh was not only tough but rigorous and painful. Again, it looked impossible with two children and a harsh economy.

As I interacted with people, everyone thought I was intelligent. I had longed stopped seeing myself as being so. As a matter of fact, I was going to settle for marriage, be a wife, serve my husband, bear children and raise them; I had no other ambition after I graduated from university. My dad died just when I set out for the mandatory national youth service. The illness was protracted, I had to see myself through the university. His strength had failed him. He could not even make much input into my life at that point. I got my first job and wanted to go back to school. If everyone said I was intelligent, then I must be. I should get back to school and get a doctorate degree. It was in this process that Charles appeared in my life and we got married not long after. Charles did not want a working wife. He wanted a submissive, silent partner. This fitted my aimless life at the time, after all, my mum was a stay-at-home mum. I thought I could fit into his wife mould. I tried. I gave it my best shot but I was suffocating. I believe that I was a late bloomer. I allowed myself sip through life. At university I did not socialise. I went to school from my parent's home. We could not afford to pay the hostel fees. Sometimes, I trekked to school and when I had money, I took a cab. I organised coaching classes for some students at a paltry sum. I sold sachet water; I did whatever would give me money besides hawking sex.

Here was I, a wife with no direction. A wife whose only desire was to please her man. I guess he must have been bored, because I was. I began to make efforts to escape his prison. I tried to get a job and earn some money to lead a better life but he was constantly in my way. His dream wife had to be a sit-at-home woman. We never discussed it, we never had such an agreement before or after marriage. Intermittently during quarrels, he muttered words that gave me an inkling of his desire. We both had mental problems if you asked me. We were two grown adults who could not face our realities. We could not discuss what we wanted and find means to make progress from where we were. We barely got by, one day at a time. Our relationship suffered, our affection doused. Hatred began to bloom. I could not tell him and I could not even face it for myself. Then the children came…

I knew I could not raise sound children in my unhappy state. The more I tried, the more Charles and I misunderstood each other, the more we clashed, the more the children were exposed to our constant nagging, the more I appeared horrible in their eyes. Things were falling apart, nothing was supporting anything. I went to the pastor, "your husband needs to affirm you, you cannot be said to be a Christian without his affirmation. He is your closest testimony, whatever he says about you is valid". This was supposed to be his encouragement without knowing he was further stabbing me. I was dying slowly, mentally, emotionally and spiritually. How could one in such a state get involved in spiritual activities? I spent every minute of my time thinking of how to please this impossible character I called my husband, the more I tried, the more I failed.

I had a mindset that marriage was a woman's ultimate achievement. It was her crown, if she lost it, she may appear not just ugly, but incomplete. I flaunted being married, I showed-off my wedding band! Looking back, I can say that it was a cover-up. I used marriage to cover up my inadequacies but in every area I fell short of expectation. My heart yearned to be free but my body suppressed it. One part of me wanted to enjoy the world with its bliss; the other was willing to stay, stuck in the religious cage. The latter won for a long time and eventually gave way. It is unlikely that a person can go so far being what she is not. I wondered who sold me the lies I lived. My mother did not work, she sewed our clothes and did her home keeping work well enough. She barely finished primary school so she had to struggle with reading, writing and interacting in English. Perhaps this must have caused her to suffer an inferiority complex. As children, we did not understand but as an adult, I believe I could relate.

Sometimes, I wondered who I patterned my life after. My dad was a workaholic. We hardly saw him while growing up. He gave us a comfortable life, we had many cars, good clothes, an abundance of food. We stopped being tenants before I was ten years old. He had landed properties that we were still selling and living on long after his demise. My mum did not have a stint for trading. She believed in acquiring properties. She bought a lot of gold and was the brain behind my dad's many lands and houses. She knew how to push. I recall when my elder brother finished university, mum wanted him to leave the shores of our nation. She pushed my dad until he got him a visa to an African country. The plan was to start from there. My brother was too fearful to leave home. He lacked the courage to swim in unknown waters. Mum was disappointed, and so were we. I loved my mum's push, she would have made a great coach, motivating people, talking, pushing. She believed that it was in our success that her success lay. She probably would have done more and achieved more if she had been more enlightened or had an enabling environment. She told us the sad story of how she had to be married off even before she knew what menstruation was. Poverty was top of the reasons for her early trade-off. My dad, a handsome, educated promising man became the lucky owner of the beautiful virgin. Their marriage was not exemplary. I grew up seeing a lot of banter, exchange of blows, a lot of unfaithfulness and infidelity. My heart always broke. My parents bad-mouthed each other and we had no option than to take sides with whoever brought the case first. Thinking back, I would not recommend such a home for a child to grow up in. It was filled with bickering and malice. I wished they were separated or divorced. I know that if mum tried it, she would have met a brick wall. Women were not as empowered as they are now. She had no valid reason to leave going by the societal expectations of her time. Was that not part of the reason Aunty Geraldine died?

Many years later, I had to tolerate some of physical and emotional abuse that mum and Aunty Geraldine had had to put up with. I was hushed and my voice was inconsequential but I was better than my aunt, she did not speak out. She died. With mum and dad, I'm quick to believe they outgrew this stage. A school of thought suggested that abuse was inevitable in a new marriage especially because the parties were just setting out. The responsibility to make the relationship work was left solely with the woman; she was to persevere and preserve the home until things worked out. This is enough to break the strongest woman, especially when the man was abusive. The thought of being responsible to clean another adult's mess in the name of preserving a marriage is burdensome, the act is onerous and depressive and can lead to irreparable damage. Little wonder many married women here are overly aggressive at work, with their children, with their children's caregivers and teachers. Quiet often, a lot of them look glossy and glamourous from a distance, but closer interaction opens up a nearly insane person. Our women bottle up so much!

I got married unsure of what I really wanted out of life and what value I was bringing to my world. Some people figure this out early in their lives, I envied them. I recall my friend Osaze. We were best of friends in our teenage years. She was an intelligent girl; we both hinged our hope on being medical doctors before we lost touch. I inquired of her many years later to learn she had studied law. There were many others like her, some were like me, they went on to marry and had no direction, while some were diehard career women having chains of businesses. By the time Charles and I were no more, I regretted most detours I'd made in life. This regret left me pacing between progression and retrogression, it left me shrunken and in despair. It further dwindled the dim hope I had in myself.

Having a poor sense of self-worth may have contributed largely to my situation. I had no faith in myself or in my abilities. I did not think I could fly. I did not think I was good enough. I saw myself as undeserving of the best things of life. I did not imagine that I could be anything, except a man made it possible. I depended on a man, my husband, and in his true nature as a man, he failed. His failing me made a resounding bang in my sub-conscious. It woke me up rudely and left me awake.

8

I Found my Therapist

In the midst of all the confusion that was threatening to overwhelm and drown me, on a quiet evening after I had just finished showering and needed to relax my nerves, I took my phone to surf through social media. This had become my favourite past time activity. I rarely watched television and when I wasn't hustling, my phone was my closest company. This was a form of relaxation for me. I simply recline on the couch and read through different updates on Facebook, LinkedIn, Instagram, twitter and what have you. I was scrolling through my newsfeed when I saw a post shared by a friend. The first sentence of the post was about self-esteem and it piqued my interest. I clicked on the main post and began to read. The writer was explaining how negative self-esteem ruined romantic relationships. I was so engrossed that I didn't even take note of the writer's name.

It was a very interesting and educative article. At the end of the fairly long post, I checked to know the particulars of the author. I did not stop there. I proposed to make contact with him. His post spoke to me, word by word, line by line. I clicked on his profile and read what I could about him. On his page, it was boldly written that he was an emotional healer and a therapist. Something clicked in my soul. "This must be the man I have been seeking" I thought to myself. I scrolled down his page and started reading his articles. I was blown away by his life changing articles. I knew the answer to my problems had come. Two hours went by, I was still reading his work. I was like a thirsty soul drinking from the fountain of life. By the time I'd had my fill with doses of his work, I was certain my healing journey had begun. He was ministering to my soul. He wasn't judging me. He wasn't belittling me. He rather healed me. It felt like he wrote all those articles for me. They were like letters written to a future lover. I felt honoured, honoured by a man I'd never met.

I couldn't contain the excitement from his wall. I sent him a friend request immediately even though I saw from his profile he had so many followers and may not have space to accept my request. I didn't allow that to deter me, I was determined. After sending the friend request to him, I quickly sent a short message.

> *"Hi sir, I have spent the last three hours on your page and I can't quantify the amount of knowledge I gained. You are amazing and full of great insights. I love what you do and I hope that you will help me with emotional issues. Kindly let me know how I can access your services. Kind regards."*

I clicked on the send icon on my Facebook messenger chat box and watched silently as my message was delivered to him.

For the next couple of hours, I was constantly checking my messenger to see if he had responded. I knew he was a very busy man, so I was really hoping that he would have the time to attend to me. I went back to his page and dropped a few comments on some of his posts. This was intended to get his attention, it worked! He responded to my comment and of course, I was as exhilarated as could be. It felt like someone had shot a load of oxytocin, dopamine and serotonin into my system. I was almost exploding with happiness. I began panting like someone who had just finished a marathon sex session. The feeling was out of this world! Instantly, my mind drifted and I began to imagine what it would feel like when he was done working on my emotions. I became even more convinced that he was the right man for the job at hand. I went to that post and told him that I had sent a message earlier. He responded and told me that he would check his inbox and respond. I was overjoyed, because it was like a dream come true. I was certain that other people on his Facebook page at that time wouldn't have known how much that comment meant to me. It also convinced me that he wasn't an arrogant person. This was a young man that had multitudes following him and was still humble enough to respond to me, an ordinary me. Infact I was going to celebrate.

Two minutes later a Facebook messenger chat head appeared on my phone screen. I saw the first name and it was his name. I promptly tapped the name and the message opened.

"Hello Ijendu, good afternoon. How are you today?"

"Good Afternoon Sir, I'm fine and hoping to be better with your help."

"All right, what do you need counselling on?"

"My emotional life is a rollercoaster right now. I feel like if I don't get the help I need, I'm headed for doom. I need counselling and therapy. Since I walked out of my marriage, I haven't been myself. My whole life seems to be in shambles. I feel terrible about myself. It is even difficult for me to find love. It seems everybody that comes to me, just wants sex from me. I have been trying to manage it but right now I can no longer hold myself together, I need help. I have read your articles and I also know that you are an emotional healer. I'm convinced that you can help me."

"Did you go through therapy after you left your marriage?

"No, I didn't."

"I see. Well, it is important that after walking out of an abusive relationship or marriage, you should get therapy. Abuse is very subtle. Most times, you wouldn't know the extent of the damage that has been done to you until you get therapy. It is not enough to walk away from the abuse. There are always aftereffects of abusive relationships. Therapy helps you deal with them and heal. If you don't heal, you will not find true happiness, even after leaving the abusive partner. You also cannot depend on time to heal you. Healing has to be deliberate."

"Apparently, this is why I have been having these issues in my life. I haven't healed. I seem to be living under the influence of my past marital experiences. Please help me, sir."

"I will help you."

"Thank you, but what will it cost me?"

"Kindly send me your email address, let me forward my service brochure to you."

I was quick to send my email address to him.

"Thank you, you will receive my email in a few minutes. Then you can get back to me after making a choice of which service to go for."

"Thank you so much"

"You are welcome, Ijendu, your best life is about to begin."

I was really happy that I'd had that conversation with him. Truly, he was right about the issues he raised. I haven't healed. I'm still very bitter about my past. I am also bitter about the men who tried to take advantage of me. I don't even know what I deserve anymore. Hopefully, this healer will save me from this terrible situation. I opened my email to see his brochure. I read through all his services and immediately chose the one-month therapy package. The fee wasn't as high as I feared it would be. It was within my budget. I replied to his email and told him the package I wanted. In the next few hours we had email exchanges that ended in me getting his bank account details. I made a quick transfer; he sent me another form to fill. I was enthralled with his organization and modus operandi. I filled the form. In the form, I was required to input my personal details and also the date and time of our first therapy session. There was an option for physical sessions, but I didn't want to meet him in person. I chose the online option. I loved the anonymity. I feared I might not be free with him if I met him in person. This had nothing to do with him. It was about the state of my mind, especially after my previous encounters with other men. I knew he was good at his job, but I was also a bit skeptical because he was a man; and men had already failed me in so many ways. These sentiments were going to change soon, because during the course of our sessions I realized he was a professional to the core. It made me respect him so much. I submitted the form after choosing the date and time of my session.

I felt really happy that I found this healer. After Dr

Emmanuel's advice that I should see a therapist, I was really worried about getting one, since therapy wasn't really common in this part of the world. I also felt limited, knowing that I wouldn't be able to have a real relationship until I had seen a therapist. It wasn't farfetched, why so many people were emotionally damaged in this society. Nobody talks about therapy the way it should be talked about. I recalled that a very enlightened colonel had earlier tried to dissuade me from seeing a therapist. He was not alone, Sonia did not consider it a need neither did Nafisat. Essien was the worst. He told me that all I needed was in him. I stopped asking their opinions long before I stumbled on this emotional healer. I mean if someone as enlightened as the colonel could try to discourage me from seeking therapy, what then is the hope of the common man or woman? The healer rightly said it that I will not be truly happy if I don't find healing. I couldn't wait to begin my sessions with him. I believed a whole new chapter was about to begin in my life.

9

MY HEALING EXPERIENCE

"**G**OOD EVENING, IJENDU. HOW ARE YOU today?" I received this message on my Skype and when I looked at the sender, I saw the name – The Emotional Healer. I almost screamed out of excitement. I was expecting his message, but it didn't occur to me that it was time for our session. I thought our session would begin by 8 pm but the message came by 7pm. I quickly checked the form I submitted and realized that I had filled in 7 pm. I put myself in character immediately and began to type a response. "Good evening, Sir. I am doing well. I hope you are well too?"

"Yes, I am. Thank you, Ijendu. Can we begin our session?"

"Yeah, sure. I'm excited about this."

"All right. So, tell me about your marriage experience. We will start from there."

I began to write a summary of my journey into matrimony and the subsequent abuse that I encountered. I wasn't worried that he would judge me. I didn't even care. My marriage meant a whole lot to me. When it collapsed, it felt like my life collapsed with it. From the upbringing I had, a woman's marriage was the ultimate symbol of her success and worth. I would have given anything for that marriage to survive. Being out here alone doesn't exactly make sense to me. But it is a burden I must bear. Perhaps there was something I didn't do right. I believed this therapist would point it out to me. Charles wasn't the best husband but it is a woman's responsibility to make her marriage work. At least that was what I was taught. I failed as a woman. I wasn't even sure I would get over this.

I narrated my experiences from the beginning of my marriage to Charles till the end. When I was done, I heaved a sigh, hoping that the therapist wouldn't hear me. Of course, he wouldn't because we were many states apart. This was one of the beauties of online counselling. It afforded maximum anonymity, even from the Counsellor. I didn't need to feel awkward about my outbursts during the course of the session. He probably didn't detect my mood, or maybe he did.

"Ijendu", typed the healer.

The message popped up on my phone. It was like the healer was reading my mind and sensed that I was drifting away with wild thoughts. My attention was drawn immediately to our session.

"Hello, sir. I'm here" I giggled.

"Your story is touching. I must also say that the foundation of your marriage was faulty from your end. You went into marriage with a wrong notion of what marriage was and how it affects you as a woman.

"Hmmmmmm!"

"Yes. Marriage is not actually all there is to a woman's life. A woman's worth is not determined by her marital status. There are lots of women who do not feel the need to get married and they are not in any way inferior to those who are married. It is a matter of choice."

My eyes were almost popping out of their sockets as I read what the healer was sending across. This was totally different from the orientation I had about marriage. Blasphemy! How could he say marriage is a matter of choice? Or, hold on a second; this is the first time somebody is telling me something different from what I believed marriage should be. Have I been shooting myself in the foot all this while? That means I didn't need marriage to validate my worth as a woman? You've got to be kidding me. So, I endured all that abuse for nothing? Oh my God!

"Ijendu, what were the forms of abuse you experienced in your marriage?"

"There was physical violence, sexual abuse, psychological, verbal and emotional abuse."

"Was there financial abuse?"

"What do you mean by financial abuse?"

"Were you earning an income during the course of your marriage? Did you have a job or business or anything that brought in personal income for you?"

"Haaaa! I didn't ooooo! My husband was against such. He didn't want me to work or do anything. He wanted me to stay at home and be a good and submissive wife to him. Well, at that point it was what I wanted. My life had no clear-cut direction. Charles came and maintained status quo. I didn't have anything of worth to do with my life.

"I understand. But you were actually going through financial abuse, that you enabled by yourself. When a man tells you not to work and make personal money, it is financial abuse. He is taking away your power to earn and have financial freedom. It puts you at a disadvantage and in a vulnerable position.

"Waoooo! Nobody told me this. I'm just learning this now. In retrospect, I wish I actually had a source of income. It would have minimized some of my negative experiences both in the hands of Charles and other men I encountered after him."

"We will address all the other forms of abuse that you experienced and you will find complete healing from them."

"Thank you, sir."

"Have you had a relationship since you left your husband?"

"Yes sir, I had a couple of relationships but none worked out. I wasn't really happy. I always felt empty, like there was something missing. The last guy even advised me to go for therapy."

"All right. I asked because you wouldn't have been able to keep a healthy relationship, without going through healing therapy first. When you walk out of an abusive relationship, what you need is not another relationship. At that point you are not emotionally fit to be in another relationship. What you need is healing. You must heal and find yourself before you get involved with another person."

"Well, I didn't know this. Men were coming my way. Some were offering me financial support, which I needed at that time."

"It is understandable. However, it is not too late to find the healing you need, which is why we are here. At this point in your life, your self-love is low, your self-esteem is negative, you have so much insecurity, there is bitterness in your soul. You have been wounded and disappointed. The work we will do will be systematic.

I will help you build your self-love, boost your self-esteem and help you become secure and confident in yourself. I will expunge the bitterness and angst in your soul and show you how to live life happily, and on your own terms. If you don't deal with all I have listed, you won't get better and time won't also help you. Time doesn't heal. What you do with time is what determines if you will be healed or if your wounds will fester."

I guess this was why it never worked. I always had this suspicion about men. After all I had been through in the hands of Charles, it was difficult for me to bestow any degree of trust on any man. They are always looking for ways to exploit vulnerable women. Prayer did it to me, Pastor, lawyer. They all took advantage of me. Or maybe they didn't. Maybe it was what I presented myself as. I wasn't really resolute about my decisions. They didn't force anything on me. I made my decisions. I accepted them. They offered me something I felt I needed. I could have said no. I had the power to say no. I accepted. In fact they might have exploited my peculiar circumstances, but I still had the power to turn them down. It wasn't entirely their fault.

I need to stop seeing myself as a weak woman who was at the mercy of all and sundry. I'm not exactly weak. I had the power of choice. I used it. Even after my healing, people will always look for loopholes to exploit me. It is my responsibility to look out for myself and protect myself from such exploitation.

"Ijendu."

"Sir." (It appeared he knew when I drifted).

"Don't judge yourself harshly. Most of our actions are a product of what we know and how we implement what we know. You will take responsibility for your own mistakes but don't judge yourself harshly. Be lenient with yourself."

"Hmmmm! All right, sir."

"Who are you angry at?"

"Charles, all those men I encountered at the end of my marriage and myself."

"All right. We will address each person and the reasons for your anger towards him. Finally, we will address your anger towards yourself. Why are you angry at Charles?"

"So many reasons. He abused me and further trampled my self-worth. He treated me like trash and hurt me in so many ways. I lost my dignity as a woman while married to him. Your question is bringing back memories that I thought had gone extinct."

"They didn't go anywhere. You only succeeded in pushing them to your inactive memory because they were hurtful and you didn't want to keep reliving them. But we need to confront them and deal with them, so that they will lose their power to hurt you."

"I was a very submissive woman to him. I thought that by being submissive I would earn his love and he would treat me right. But he didn't. He abused and treated me with scorn. I hate him for everything he did to me. I'm sorry I'm venting."

"Don't feel sorry. Your emotions at this moment are very legitimate. Don't hold back. Let it flow. If you keep it back it will become poisonous and harmful to you. You need to expel every toxic element of that experience. You can't afford to keep them within you."

"Thank you, Sir."

"We will address all the reasons for your anger towards Charles, individually. No stone will be left unturned. When we are done with Charles, we will look into your reasons for being angry with those other men, before we address your anger with yourself."

"All right, sir."

"This is where our session will end today. Before our next session, I want you to make a list of everything that Charles did to offend you. Then make a list of the things you are angry with yourself about. This therapy is in stages and each stage is meant to address a particular aspect of your life. So, we have to address everything responsible for the pains and bitterness in your soul."

"Thank you, I feel relieved. Looks like a burden has been lifted off me. I will write a list of all the things you asked me to write."

"Perfect."

"Goodnight sir."

"Goodnight Ijendu."

"Pheeew!" This was awesome indeed. Finally, my healing journey had begun. My heart felt lighter. It felt good to have someone to vent to without fear of judgement. I really couldn't wait to have the next session with him.

10

LOVING THE JOURNEY

"I LOVE YOU MUMMY," THEY BOTH ECHOED.

"I love you more," I answered as I hugged them tightly.

"You are the best mummy in the whole wide world," said my daughter.

"Yes, www best mummy," concurred my son.

"I have to be, I just have to be, you both deserve a great mum, don't you?"

I bought a cake, got some drinks, made different dishes and tagged the party 'new me'. I deemed it necessary to celebrate the new found me after going through therapy and implementing a few ideas from the therapist. I began to feel new and think differently. I started to live consciously and to carry myself with some dignity, the therapist had taught me what abuse was and how much power I had given my abusers. They wielded the powers I allowed them indiscriminately against me. The end result was the wreck I became and it was impossible to raise healthy children. Knowing as much as I knew, it was time for a rebirth. With each day's success, I thought I could have a celebration in honour of the 'new me'. I tried to explain to the children the essence of what I was up to and how I hoped they would not walk the path I had walked. Even though they both nodded in affirmation, I hoped they understood. They were not the focus at the time, I was. I was learning to take things a step at a time with me and with everyone else. The children and I partied hard. We drank, ate, danced, hugged and spoke kind words, one to another. We talked about our lives before and made some projections about our expectations henceforth. We were going to work as a team; we would respect one another more and remain kind regardless of the situation. We were going to be loving, speak lovingly and bear our burdens. We were genuinely happy. For a second, I saw my children as adults in their own right. The journey of single parenting became lighter and more interesting. The party was needed, thanks to the therapy. I took some time to tell my children what had happened to me, how I had dealt with it and the stage I was at. I apologized for the times I had screamed at them. I committed to being a better mum and that we will walk hand in hand through the journey of single parenting. Gratefully, they are teenagers, they understood some of my pain and aches.

An early evening on the last week of the year, I was having a telephone chat with Sonia. We shared our high and low moments for the year and as our manner was, encouraged each other. Sonia is a relentless woman. From her actions and reactions, it seems she did not know the meaning of distraction, discouragement and obstacle. She had three boys to care for. Her ex-husband had moved in with another woman leaving her to walk the path of parenting alone. She braced up to the challenges, showing no angst. "What if he was dead, would I not raise my boys?" she would always ask. She was in her seventh year as a single mum when our paths crossed. She was not this phlegmatic from the onset. She had her rough times then lived through it. "I'm now a diamond" she said to me. Because we had been friends for a few years, we had caught up on each other's strengths, weaknesses and plans. We found time to update ourselves on our children and our men, present and past.

"Your children will have a step sibling soon" Sonia said to me.

"Really? Congrats to them"

"It seems she will have the baby abroad"

"Lucky her then, they can enjoy"

"This is a better you girl, I wasn't sure whether to tell you or not"

"Indeed, I'm getting better every day. We have to accept what we cannot change, that's the serenity prayer isn't it?" I added.

We moved on to other topics. Sonia and I broached as many topics as we could. We had different personalities, when I think of how we get along, I jolt. I feel cheery about it. Our conversation about my kids having a step sibling did not feel like the news of his wedding. This was one sure sign that I was on a healthy path, I was healing and becoming progressive. I was proud of myself. She showed me the pictures and I was truly happy for Charles' new wife. She looked happy and well cared for. I muttered a prayer for her and the unborn baby. My heart was without guile towards her. "Lord, make this happiness beyond social media, amen" I prayed again before switching to another subject. "My friend has changed" Sonia said, "what happened to you? When, where, how? Tell me what happened to you baby girl".

I knew why she was insisting that something happened to me. Some eighteen or so months earlier, she had broken the news of Charles' wedding to me. It was a Sunday night while we were having one of our 'catch-up' moments. I changed the tide.

"Babes, I saw you're friends with a certain Cassandra on Facebook."

"Yeah, I follow her."

"She is my ex's current."

"Really? She is married now."

"Wow, she must have dumped him."

"Her wedding trended, it was a few months ago, wait let me check."

As I waited, I was scrolling through my phone, responding to messages and keeping busy. Suddenly, the pictures flooded my phone, the traditional and the church wedding.

"What!!! That's my ex," I exclaimed.

"Really?"

"Yes, we are not even divorced. We have not even appeared in court and he has wedded?"

I dropped the phone and…Sonia called.

I said I was strong. I talked tough and bragged like a big girl. I hid my exasperation. I thought I was in control. As soon as Sonia felt I was alright, she hung up. I had myself to contend with. I took my time to go through the pictures, every bit of them became important. The smiles, poses, clothes, make-up, background, every single thing the camera captured had to be analysed. I began to forward the pictures to friends and family. I needed to show them that there was no more reason to hold back or wait as they advised. The pictures were enough evidence that I should move on which I always canvased for. Most of them replied, others called with words of encouragement. Ify in particular, called and sang songs of praise with me. She was more excited than I was, urged me to be grateful to God. Nothing sounded more foolish to me that night. I refused to sing along, she persuaded me. I was as irritated as I was buoyant. Looking back, I imagine the state of my heart that night. I slept peacefully or so I thought.

The next morning, I could not get ready for work. I managed to take a shower, to get dressed, and take a taxi to the office. It was about 8:00am when I started palpitating… I could not work. I was looking at the pictures and doing critical analysis; call it jealousy or envy. It may have been pride or arrogance. "She's a cute girl *sha*" I said to myself "But I fine pass her". I compared my height and shape and complexion. "*Dis* one *na* make-up *jor* but her boobs *na wah ooo*" I was still musing. I usually do not speak in broken English, it is not my style. This was the first indication that I was losing it! "Idiot man, foolish fool, I wonder how he deceived this small *geh.*" I was hating on him. Suddenly... Sweat oozed down my face. I sneezed and coughed. I became frigid. I temporarily blacked out with my head feeling like it was in a three hundred- and sixty-degree spin. Then I blinked my eyes and pinched myself. I was still alive.

"What just happened?" I asked me.

I made to stand, I stood but then I could not sit. When I eventually did, I could not talk. I could not eat nor drink. My pulse beat faster and faster. I went back to the pictures and even the video. It was a classy wedding by all accounts. My hands started shaking. I was shaking all over, and I was alone in the office. My office door was closed. Everywhere was silent. Who do I tell? What do I do? What was happening? I had no answers. I did not realise what was causing the problem. The pictures I was looking at were spinning in my head. I knew I had to call for help. I sent a message to Sonia. "Help, I can't move, I can't breathe." I could feel my heart beat slowing. I placed my head on my desk unsure of what next to do. I said my last prayers and closed my eyes …

I understood why Sonia thought I had changed. I did not tell her my voyage with the therapist. Indeed, it was a journey! In all, I was excited that what was happening inwards was manifesting outwardly. My closest friend was beginning to see my growth, the changes were clear. I had to pat myself on the back. This was satisfying.

Ify was following up on me. She liked the new vibes I gave out. She was my number one fan.

Ide, my lovely son was beginning to relax with me. I was no longer snapping at him at the slightest mistake. Ide was a quiet boy; my constant nagging made him withdraw into his shell. We rarely conversed. When he was not at school, doing school work, he was in front of the television or computer. As much as I was worried about this, I had relatively no control over it. I was traumatized with no help. I knew it, I knew that I was spewing hot and cold, it was not a good sign. I knew that turning to men for money was completely against my principles, my upbringing and everything I stood for. I knew that I was derailing, I had to be out of my mind to be on that path. For each time I exhibited this alien behaviour, something I could not explain always reprimanded me. "This is not you, you know", I always heard this in my subconscious. I argued with this voice daily, I never gave in until I met the therapist. My children got the short side of the stick most often. They were the first to get a sarcastic answer to their questions "Mum, where are you off to?" "Will staying at home put food on the table?" was one of my replies. They gave up asking. On the surface, we looked 'cool' but I knew we were far from the picture we portrayed. I recall how Charles and I always put up a 'perfect couple' picture while we haboured malice.

I was delighted to sit with Ide to watch television and discuss his thoughts about what he had watched. I was happy to watch him painting on his computer. It was a pleasure to hear him talk about his friends and their escapades at school. He freely discussed his feelings for a girl, the hair in his penile area, and how he would not like to have a beard. "I like this mum" he told me. I smiled as I replied "your mum is back, stronger and better for you!" We had the tightest of hugs and kisses. I loved my son dearly, tears streamed down my eyes; I didn't know what to make of this reunion. It was grand to me. I didn't know how wide a gulley had existed between my son and I. Due to his quiet nature, one could have easily sworn that we were doing alright. Looking back, it's exhilarating to have sought for help, else how would I have explained what my son deteriorated to? His endless hugs afterwards made me ponder what he was going through as well. It could not have been easy watching the family he knew disintegrate. It must have been tough on his young mind. If only I had a 'mind-o-meter' to gauge what went on there. He brought up the struggles he had with peers when they enquired the whereabout of his dad. I felt his pain, but maybe not the entire pain. I imagined how the smile on his face fizzled out once his classmates mentioned dad. It must have been a bitter and caustic pill to swallow. I felt guilty for putting him through this trauma. He didn't deserve it; no child deserves it. Parents should rather do better in this regard. Surely separation can be less painful!

I opened up my heart to more people and more love, I noticed my pool of friends skyrocketing. The assertion that man is a social animal was evident in my story. I had always been a 'people-person'. I prefer to be with people and lending a helping hand. It was no longer for what I would get but for what I could give. Sex for money was completely eliminated. I worked with a clearer mindset. I believed more in myself and my abilities. I ran with my strengths and abandoned my weaknesses. I paid no attention to distractions, changed my circle of friends to non-judgmental people. For the first time in many years, I began to glow, my skin, my speech, my style.

Being a single parent, I was the sole decision maker in matters concerning the children and me. I finally saw the positive side of this – quick decision making. I loved the fact that I had to trust my sense of judgement. I had earlier deceived myself about needing a male perception to things. On the contrary, it was a feeling of incompleteness and inadequacy that made me hinge on 'male-perspective'. Surely, there is a male perspective to things, but then in the absence of a male, I simply had to believe in myself enough to make the right decision for the family. I took this bold step, I was happy I did. I still seek male opinions but no, they do not validate me. They are not more important than mine. They are simply another angle but not a superior angle. Being single did not mean being incomplete, I was single and I was a complete being. I began to enjoy the journey, the journey of single parenting. It is a beautiful and adventurous expedition, why did I not see this all along?

"Mum, guess what I'm wearing?" grinned my daughter hiding behind the curtain.

"Well, if you come out, I will see and then make a guess" I answered her.

She came out grinning from ear to ear …

"Wow, this is beautiful, you mean my top suits you? Someone is a big girl!"

She must have been surprised. Her old mum would have screamed for touching her clothes. I would have reminded her how I was making do with my few clothes and how she should have remembered that I'm her mum and an adult and all the rantings. It was easier to be joyful than to be irksome. Our family was beaming again, we were truly together void of anger and bitterness. "My baby, I'm excited you are growing, feel free, my wardrobe is yours. Enjoy it!" I gave her the go ahead. My daughter gave me another tight hug. This, I considered a pure form of showing love. When your child expresses this form of love, it is worth more than a million naira.

I sat down one evening and in sober reflection, I questioned the core of what I believed. I had to build my values again. If I was not a prostitute, why have sex for money? If I were to have sex for money, would that not be business and if it was business, how much should I be paid and in what manner should my business be executed, who calls the shots?

Sex was only pleasurable in the first few years of marriage. Afterwards, it declined until it became a chore and finally, it was just routine. I knew that love died. I must have been on a vengeance mission with myself. An evaluation was necessary having seen the emotional doctor. Anything that did not sit well in my sub-conscious became a value to me. I did not continue to be a city without walls. It was my belief that everyone should have and stick with ideals. Ideals make one live purposefully.

Epilogue

LIFE TRULY BEGINS WHEN A WOMAN wholeheartedly accepts things that she cannot change. Prior to that it would be toss and turn without direction. Money and anything else are unable to create self-love, self-validity and self-acceptance. All that took place became my story. I had to embrace it, I had to make it part of my history regardless of how despicable it was. My story is my history, my history is my experience, my experience empowers me to be true and in doing so, I am able to offer help to others in my stead.

With self-love, came true happiness which in turn made me able to decipher a good intention from a negative one. It is not in the place of a lover to heal a broken partner. A broken partner should get help from a therapist before walking into a new relationship. This way, there is an assurance of wholeness and a leveled foundation.

I continued dating Mike as a happy woman. There were relapses a few times but it was quickly contained. Mike had been through what I had. He handled things differently. According to him, he counted his loss as soon as it dawned on him that things weren't working. For him, it was a great loss. He invested everything – money, time, energy, friends, name it, he invested everything he thought would help him make his marriage worthwhile. He spared nothing. He was happy to make the investments, he was optimistic. He was focused and could afford to. One after the other, he saw his sweat yield no fruit. He saw his dream of a great home with Pat crashing. The crash was so terrible that nothing was saved. He cried. A man hardly cried, he remembered his dad's warning about being a man at all times and held himself. He tried to stay strong as hurtful as it was. He hoped against all hope until the inevitable happened. Pat walked out without looking back. The lavish wedding was nothing. The money spent training her to become a doctor was a waste, she did not become a doctor. She kept failing. He took solace in the fact that he gave his best. Posterity will judge him fairly so he believed. I promised Mike that I would write his story. I hope I do some day.

We met at a party. The party Nnedi almost made me late for. I finally got there just before the door was shut. It was an exclusive party, admission was strictly by invitation and the door was closed fifteen minutes from the start time. I was lucky to have got in at the twelfth minute. Just as I got in, Mike was by the door.

"Hello ma'am," he said.

"Hi," I replied without raising my head.

I almost fell as I proceeded to the main bowl. My long evening gown was in the way and my stilettoes stepped on it. Mike was on hand to pick me up. I looked up, thanked him with a warm smile. I was grateful he'd saved me the embarrassment.

"Since you are alone, can I be your company?" he asked.

"Sure, you may, thank you," I was happy to oblige.

He pointed his elbow at me, I hooked in my hand and together we walked in. I was reminded of Cinderella and her Prince. Everyone thought we came together except Mike's bosom friend who brought him to the party. We looked a perfect pair. The party was the most beautiful night I'd ever had. The dancing, the drinks, the food, the discussion, the company, the networking, everything seemed planned for me. I fitted in so well amongst people I never knew. Mike completely took charge, kept me in his circle, introduced me as his bride-to-be without even a word from me. I got another job on the spot from the governor. The moment Mike introduced me to him, he asked what I did, "I'm a business manager your excellency, I'm skilled in many ways, I will bring lots of value to your administration," I replied.

"Ok then, tell Ogunsanya, my chief of staff to enlist her. I think she will make a great team member," the governor instructed Mike.

Just before Mike and I conceived Jeofrey, I shared my perspectives on life with him. He shared his too. We kept our lives as simple as we could. "There is no need complicating life, it is complex by its self" this is Mike's philosophy. I bought into it, we worked with it. One thing bothered him out of all he knew about me.

"Are you lesbian?"

"Uhhhhm"

"You are?"

"Why do you ask?"

"Please be honest, it won't affect anything I promise."

"Why do you ask then?"

"I need to know; I need to know what to expect and what not to expect. I need to know how to protect you. I need you to be mine, totally mine."

"I'm not a property to be owned Mikky."

"You know what I mean, are you lesbian, please tell me."

I heaved a deep sigh. I did not know if I was straight or not. I couldn't believe it!

"Do you want the truth Mikky?"

"Yes love, the truth please."

"I sincerely don't know, that's the truth. I have watched a lot of pornography. It's stuck in my head. Sometimes when I see a beautiful lady, my imagination runs wild. I like playing with the female body. With you, I'm in love. It's not play, I feel like laying my life for you. I feel complete with a man…"

"Thank goodness!" he exclaimed.

"Why? You did not let me finish."

"You are not, if you were, we won't be analyzing. We simply have to make sure you get enough love doses from me and before long, those creepy imaginations will fade."

Mike was right. I'm as straight as a ruler. Mike and I have a son together. We live together. We are not married. We are simply committed to each other's wholeness and happiness.

They said life is good, nothing is truer when you love yourself and are in company of people who love themselves too.

www.ingramcontent.com/pod-product-compliance
Lightning Source LLC
Chambersburg PA
CBHW061540120726
48001CB00004B/1640